JAWS OF DEATH

Joe had managed to sneak inside the lumbermill, but where was Frank? As Joe made his way through the noisy mill, he stole a glance at the enormous wood chipper at the far end of the room.

Just then a worker farther down the line bellowed, "Punch the button!" and pointed toward the gaping entrance of the chipper.

Joe swiveled around and gasped. Lying half on and half off the moving conveyer belt was a body. Joe peered through the dusty air at the motionless figure.

"Frank!"

Joe knew that the chipper could suck in massive pieces of wood and reduce them to splinters in mere seconds.

Exploding into a run, Joe raced for the mouth of the horrible machine—but he knew that his brother didn't stand a chance.

Books in THE HARDY BOYS CASEFILES™ Series

Available from ARCHWAY Paperbacks

THE HARDY BOYS CASEFILES NO. 60

DEADFALL

FRANKLIN W. DIXON

AN ARCHWAY PAPERBACK
Published by POCKET BOOKS

New York   London   Toronto   Sydney   Tokyo   Singapore

AN ARCHWAY PAPERBACK *Original*

An Archway Paperback published by
POCKET BOOKS, a division of Simon & Schuster Inc.
1230 Avenue of the Americas, New York, NY 10020

ISBN: 0-671-73096-7

First Archway Paperback printing February 1992

10 9 8 7 6 5 4 3 2 1

Cover art by Brian Kotzky

Printed in the U.S.A.

IL 6+

DEADFALL

Chapter
1

"THOSE RASPBERRY PANCAKES were the best I ever had, Stan!" Joe Hardy said as Stan Shaw's four-by-four truck bounced down a narrow, tree-lined mountain road. "What a way to start the day."

"I start practically every day like that—when the berries are in season." Stan's weathered face split into a wide grin. "Thanks to the raspberry bushes in my backyard."

Joe smiled. Though Stan was over fifty years old, the tall, lean environmentalist had the manner and build of a man half his age.

"It wouldn't matter if they were cactus bushes," remarked Joe's eighteen-year-old brother, Frank, from the cramped backseat. "Joe's the breakfast king."

"And lunch," chimed in Callie Shaw, winking at Frank next to her. "And dinner. And—"

1

"Okay, already," Joe protested. "I was just trying to compliment our host. It's not every guy who'd let a couple of strangers camp out in his house."

"You're not strangers. You're Callie's friends," Stan said, slowing the truck as the road made a tight curve. To the right, the mountain fell off into a narrow valley in which Joe glimpsed a cluster of buildings—a tiny logging village.

"That's Crosscut, Oregon—not quite as big as New York City, but it's all we've got," Stan drawled.

Seventeen-year-old Joe smiled and glanced back at his brother. Joe's muscular build and blond hair were in strong contrast to Frank's slimmer physique and brown hair. The brothers knew each other so well that each could often guess what the other was thinking.

At the moment, Joe knew, they were both remembering what Callie had told them about her uncle Stan on their flight from the East. Stan had been stationed in Crosscut for nearly ten years as a field representative of the Save the Redwoods Alliance. The local mill owners had come to tolerate his lectures on preserving endangered plant species and protecting local wildlife. Stan had felt he was making progress in helping people make a living from the forests without destroying them.

In the past couple of years, though, ecology activists from other, less responsible organizations, and even interns sent to learn from Stan, had become more aggressive, and the loggers were reacting angrily. Now it was a cold war between the environmentalists, or "Greens," and the loggers, who believed that people like Stan were out to take away their jobs. During the past year fistfights had started breaking out between some of the loggers and a group of over-eager Greens.

Though Stan had come up with several plans that offered timber to the mill owners as well as protection for animal and plant wildlife, the loggers were still convinced that he wanted to take away their jobs.

Callie decided to visit her uncle to see if she could help him, and had asked Frank and Joe to come along in case there was trouble.

Stan knew that the Hardys' father, Fenton, was a well-known private investigator, and that the boys were also amateur detectives. He probably figured that the Hardys weren't there just to hike and enjoy the scenery. But if he wanted to pretend that Joe and Frank were ordinary visitors, that was fine with them.

"Here we are," Stan announced as the truck reached the bottom of the mountain. The village of Crosscut swung into view once again. "I'll stop in at the general store. You kids can easily walk from there to the foot of Cascade Trail."

"Wow." Joe took in the three-block stretch of buildings set against the tree-covered mountains. "The town looks kind of lost with those giant mountains in the background."

3

Faded wooden signs indicated the Potbelly Café and Tichman's Grocery, which were separated by a shoe repair shop with a gaudy neon sign. On the other side of the street were the Crosscut General Store and the Sportsman's Pool Hall.

"We didn't get to see much on our way in from the airport last night. This looks like real backwoods territory," Joe said.

"Don't count on it," Stan said with an edge to his voice. "Folks here are more savvy than you think." He parked the truck in front of the general store. "Looks like we've got a lot of laid-off loggers hanging around waiting to prove it, too."

"Laid off?" Joe and Stan climbed out of the truck, followed by Frank and Callie.

Stan nodded toward a mud-spattered red pickup sitting in a row of battered station wagons and four-wheel-drive vehicles. "See that pickup?" he asked. "It belongs to Buster Owens, owner of the Horizon Lumber Mill out on Highbridge Road. He's shut his mill down for two weeks, starting today. He says he can't afford to keep operating with his old equipment, so he's stopping all work while he rerigs the mill. He has the loggers on half pay in the meantime, and they're not happy about it."

"And when they're not happy," Callie added grimly, "they tend to take out their frustrations on guys like Uncle Stan."

Stan shrugged resignedly and started up the

wooden steps. Joe and Frank and Callie followed close behind.

"Wow," Frank said as they entered the store. "Just like in the movies."

Joe looked around the room. It *was* a little like the set of a western film. One half of the large, warehouselike building was crammed full of shelves displaying everything from snack food to bolts of cloth. A short, wiry man in a worn corduroy jacket sat behind a cash register and appeared to be working on his accounts. The town post office, with its gleaming brass mailboxes, was set up along the back wall. To the right, a heavyset woman, who Joe guessed was married to the man in the corduroy jacket, rushed about refilling coffee cups for a collection of rough-looking men at the lunch counter.

"Yeah, but this smells better than a movie," Joe said, inhaling the rich, greasy aroma of bacon and eggs. Joe eyed the men in their worn jeans, faded plaid shirts, and heavy boots. The men had noticed Stan and his guests, but so far they'd only glared and turned back to their coffee.

"Hey there, Will," Stan said, nodding to the man behind the cash register. Then he focused on the men eating breakfast and gave one of them a casual wave. "Buster! How's it going?"

Joe noted which of the men waved back. The mill owner was a big man—over six feet tall and could be over three hundred pounds. He wore a lime green cap with a purple-and-orange Horizon logo, jeans, and a flannel shirt, as most of the other men were, but hanging from his wide leather belt was the largest key ring Joe had ever seen.

"Uncle Stan thinks he's got Buster nearly ready to try some new logging methods," Callie murmured to Joe and Frank as they searched the shelves for trail mix. "But Buster still doesn't want to be friendly to him in public."

She was about to go on when the door was banged open. All three of them whirled around to see a short, balding man in a camouflage jacket race into the store. He had a brown beard and mustache and wild-looking blue eyes. "Shaw! I've been searching all over for you, man," the short man said to Callie's uncle Stan. "Let's go! We've got a major emergency!"

"Calm down, Vance," Stan said with a nervous chuckle. "What seems to be the trouble?"

"Some Horizon Lumber trucks are headed west to cut a stand of redwoods," the younger man announced excitedly, not even trying to keep his voice down. "We've got to stop them!"

Stan glanced toward the loggers with an embarrassed expression. Joe saw several of the lumbermen exchange sour looks over their food.

"Who is that guy?" Joe muttered to Callie.

"Vance Galen," Callie murmured back. "He's Uncle Stan's assistant from Save the Redwoods. Stan said he's the guy who started the fighting last summer."

Joe studied the angry, potbellied man and decided he looked a little ridiculous in his camouflage jacket. It was as though he was dressed for war when everyone else just wanted breakfast. No wonder the loggers disliked him.

"Horizon's shut down, Vance, remember?" Stan said to the room in general, trying to ease the very real tension. "Buster's right here. Why don't we ask him what's going on?"

"It's none of your business," shouted one of the loggers. He was a hefty man, a little shorter than average height, with a dark beard and mustache that covered half his face.

"Yeah!" piped up a skinny, long-haired man sitting next to him.

"We're sitting here out of work and you *still* treat us like the bad guys. I wish we *were* out there cutting down those trees!" the heftier man argued.

"That's Mike Stavisky and Freddy Zackarias," Callie murmured to the Hardys. She remembered them from the last time she had visited. "Both of them were involved in the fights last summer."

"All right, that's enough," Buster said. He set his coffee cup down and got up from his stool. Immediately, the room fell silent. Frank decided anyone that big could quiet any room.

"First of all, Vance, those trucks are on their way to my equipment yard for maintenance, not to cut trees," Buster said to the angry activist. "You should know better than anyone that not only are those redwoods protected by the state

7

of Oregon, but they're also on public land. The contract on that land has expired, and nobody's going to be cutting trees there until the Forest Service draws up a new contract."

"Since when are you so concerned about following regulations?" Vance Galen retorted. "You'd turn the state of Oregon into a parking lot if you could make a buck off it!"

"Hey, hey!" Stan shouted as the loggers began shouting insults again. "This isn't doing anyone any good. Vance here got a little overexcited, that's all, and we both apologize. We don't want any of you to lose your livelihood, you know that. We're just here to show you how you can harvest trees without destroying a national treasure."

"Trees are trees, Stan!" a logger shouted from the lunch counter.

"Maybe so," Stan replied. "But if you cut 'em all down without leaving any or at least replanting, you're going to wind up with no trees pretty quick. And then not only will the local wildlife be in big trouble, but your children, and *their* children, will be, too. How can they be loggers if there aren't any more trees?"

"Not bad," Joe heard Frank whisper to Callie. Joe watched as Callie smiled proudly at her uncle.

"The Greens aren't your problem, anyway, boys." The voice came from a man leafing through some mail by the post office. He was a tall, thin, middle-aged man with craggy features, light, wispy hair, and piercing blue eyes. In his jeans and flannel shirt he looked more like a mid-western farmer than a logger.

"Bo Johnson!" Stan called with fake heartiness. "I didn't see you back there. So, what do you think the problem is?"

"Bo owns Johnson Lumber," Callie whispered even before the Hardys could ask. "Horizon's biggest competitor."

"The problem," Johnson said, stepping toward the lunch counter and pointing with his stack of mail at the loggers, "is Horizon Lumber's management. What kind of outfit lays off its entire staff just to put in a little equipment? If you boys worked for me, you'd be out there in the woods today making top dollar instead of arguing with the likes of *him*."

Johnson gestured disdainfully toward Vance Galen. Galen turned red in the face and made a move toward the older man. "Why, you—"

"Hey!" Buster Owens put a hand up, stopping both Galen and Johnson in their tracks. Then he turned to Johnson. "What kind of trouble do you have in mind this morning, Bo? Want to start another fight? I can call in Sheriff Ferris to referee if you want."

"I didn't mean anything by it." Johnson, smiling, lifted his hands in mock surrender. His eyes slid back to the loggers, and he nodded. "I'm just saying that that Forest Service contract is going to be awarded to Johnson Lumber. And the minute we can move in to cut those trees, you fellas know where to come for work."

After giving the furious Buster a salute, Johnson strolled toward the door. "Oh, and, Stan," he added as he passed the Greens, "I may give the sheriff a call myself. Looks like your boy, Vance, needs restraining again."

"Some town," Joe commented half an hour later after he, Callie, and Frank had hit the wilderness trail. Already they were surrounded by lush, cool forest. "Is it my imagination, or were those folks incredibly uptight?"

"I warned you it wouldn't be a picnic," he heard Callie answer behind him. "It's understandable, really. Guys like Bo Johnson don't understand what Uncle Stan and the rest of the Greens are doing. And Greens like Vance Galen forget that the loggers are people who need to make a living."

"That Forest Service contract they were talking about," Frank said. "Why is it so important?"

"The private land is nearly logged out," Callie explained. "And the Greens have convinced the state government and the federal forestry people to think long and hard about the logging methods they'll allow on public land in their next contract. Stan's hoping they'll permanently forbid any cutting of redwoods and all clear-cutting."

"What's clear-cutting?" Frank asked.

"That's when loggers cut all the trees in a stand without leaving anything behind," Callie explained. "When they do that, the rain washes the topsoil away. The next thing you know, nothing can grow there. If the loggers would cut a little here, a little there, and plant a tree for every one cut down, the forests could be saved. The logging industry and the forests could go on for generations."

Joe led the way around another bend in the trail. The path was muddy from the rain the night before, and tiny streams of water trickled over the moss-covered boulders at the edge of the path and dripped down toward the valley below. Closing in on the other side of the hikers were lush ferns. From the tops of the pines, birds called loudly. It was a shame, Joe reflected, to think of these beautiful mountains stripped bare.

"If you want to see what a clear-cut field looks like, check out the view to your right," Callie cried a few minutes later, as though she'd been reading Joe's mind. They paused to peer through the trees at a large cleared area farther up on the mountainside.

"Come on, let's get a better look." Callie cut off the trail and started through the trees, Frank and Joe close behind.

Even though Callie had described what a clear-cut field was, Joe was shocked by the sight. The barren area was hundreds of yards across, littered with tree stumps and almost nothing else. No animals were in sight. Joe heard nothing but an eerie silence.

"It's like being on the moon," Frank said as they trudged across the huge expanse of wasteland.

"And this isn't the biggest strip," Callie muttered. She paused on the far side of the field. "That's Horizon Lumber down there." She pointed toward a collection of sheds, mammoth lumber piles, and heavy equipment beside a fast-moving river. "Buster Owens's mill. They carve a chunk this size out of forest every other week."

Joe peered at a lone vehicle sitting in the mill's parking lot. "Isn't that your uncle's truck?" he asked.

Callie said with surprise, "Yes, it is. I thought he had some more business to do in town. I wonder what he's doing over there?"

"Especially since the mill's shut down at the moment," Frank pointed out. "I don't see anyone moving around down there."

"And look," Joe exclaimed. "See that red truck pulled off the road behind those bushes? It looks somehow familiar."

Frank followed his brother's gaze down the river about a quarter of a mile from the factory. "It looks like Buster Owens's truck," he said. "Why would he park off the side of the road instead of at the mill?" He glanced at the others. "I think we should go see if either of them needs help."

Callie hesitated. She didn't want to ask too

much of the Hardys, but she was worried about her uncle.

"Come on," Joe said. "There must be a way across the river."

"There's a path that leads to a bridge." Callie took the lead.

Callie started down the mountain at a brisk pace, but within a few steps the three of them broke out into a run. Then, only a few minutes after that, Joe heard the sound of an enormous explosion. The great force of the blast almost knocked him off his feet.

"What was that?" Callie cried after Joe helped her to her feet.

"I can't see anything down there now." Joe stared out over the river. "But it sounded like Buster Owens's mill just blew up!"

Chapter

2

"UNCLE STAN!" Before Frank could stop her, Callie had run past him toward the river. She stumbled over a tangle of roots as Frank and Joe ran after her.

"Hold on, Callie!" Frank cried, catching up with her as they broke through the trees at the edge of the river. He stopped dead in his tracks the instant he saw the mill directly across the river. Enormous flames were consuming the center of the large main building. It was the size of a football field—designed, Frank knew, to swallow trees at one end and spit lumber, plywood, and toothpicks out at the other. Surrounding it were a number of wooden warehouses, all as frighteningly flammable as the mill.

Through the thick, black smoke Frank could just see that the roof of the mill was about to cave in.

As they stared, another explosion rocked them. The flames shot even higher, and then one of the nearby warehouses burst into flame, too. They winced at the heat that reached them even across the river. "It's burning so fast! It looks like a chemical explosion, or dynamite maybe," he shouted over the roaring of the fire.

"Do you see anyone?" Callie demanded, trying to peer through the smoke. She called her uncle's name, but Frank was sure no one could hear her from where they were.

"We're at the wrong angle to see the parking lot," Frank pointed out. "There's no way to know if he's still there."

"Let's cross the river here and try to find him," said Joe. "That fire isn't getting any smaller."

"We can't cross without a bridge," Frank said. "The current's too strong to swim, and it's too deep to wade across."

"We don't have time to go to the bridge. Look, over there!" Callie pointed to what looked like a floating forest that ran from one bank of the river to the other. "That's a log raft. When the loggers cut trees down upriver they float the logs down to here. A chain strung across the river catches them and holds them like cattle in a pen."

"You want to cross on that? It seems like a great way to end up getting wet." Frank eyed the enormous logs floating in the coursing river. There were chains on bright red floats lashed to thick posts on either bank, but the logs themselves appeared to be slick and would be dangerous to step on in the fast current.

"It's our only chance," said Callie, flinging off her pack and starting on ahead of the Hardys. "Uncle Stan could be hurt!"

Frank glanced at his younger brother. Joe shrugged. "We'd better keep up," he said, "or she'll go without us."

The brothers tossed their packs down next to Callie's and hurried after her to the edge of the river. The logs bucked and tossed on top of the rushing water. "Uncle Stan showed me how to do this last summer. I'll go first," Callie shouted over the noise of the river. Before Frank could stop her, she had half-stepped, half-slid onto the first enormous, algae-covered log. For a terrible moment Frank watched as she lost her footing, but she instantly caught herself and jumped lightly to the next rearing log.

"The secret is to keep moving," she shouted back over her shoulder.

"I'm next," Joe announced, sliding recklessly down the riverbank and barely landing on a log. When Callie was halfway across the river with Joe a few feet behind her, Frank slid down the bank to land unsteadily on a log.

This is like dancing on ice, Frank thought.

Moments later, muddy and wet from the spray of river water, Frank joined the other two on the top of the far bank.

"Let's not waste time," Joe said. "The fire's bigger. And I still don't see Stan!"

As the three of them ran toward the blazing mill, they heard a siren approaching. A moment later they spotted a fire truck through the trees. Men in everyday clothes and yellow helmets were hanging on to the sides of the truck. They looked as though they'd dropped whatever they were doing to come to fight the fire.

As the teenagers neared the mill, the parking lot came into view. "Stan's truck is gone," Frank said, relieved. "He must have left before the explosion. But wouldn't he have heard it?"

"No time to worry about that now," Joe pointed out. "This is a volunteer fire department—just the local townspeople. They could probably use our help."

"There're more volunteers coming," Callie said, pointing down the road. "In a little town like this, everybody has to pitch in." Behind the fire truck were several cars with flashing red lights stuck on to their dashboards. The drivers and passengers were staring, awestruck, at the growing blaze.

As they jogged toward the parking lot to meet the fire truck, Frank could hear the siren wailing in Crosscut, far down the mountain. At the same time another siren sounded and Frank spotted a police car racing up the mountain from the opposite direction. He wondered whether it would be the Sheriff Ferris that Stan had mentioned at the general store.

The volunteer fire fighters had piled off the truck and were unwinding the enormous fire hose and heading toward the blaze with it. Frank approached one of the men, who was already sweating under his yellow helmet. "Anything we can do to help?" he shouted over the noise of the sheriff's siren.

"Sure. Line up and help move the hose," the man commanded. "Tell the others to do the same. We think somebody might still be in there."

Callie's face went pale in spite of the incredible heat from the blaze.

Frank put an arm around her. "Remember," he cautioned, "Stan's truck is gone. There's no reason to think it's him."

Before Callie could respond another car pulled up beside the trio and a man and woman in jeans and T-shirts leapt out. "How can we help?" the woman demanded, her eyes switching from Frank to the enormous, frightening blaze.

"Help with the hose," Frank told her. "We'll need all the volunteers we can get."

By now the fire had spread throughout the mill. Two warehouses and one of the huge piles of lumber that lay at the edge of the property were also burning. More cars and trucks had arrived from town. The instant they stopped in the parking lot, loggers and other locals leapt out to help.

The sheriff was kept busy giving orders to the volunteers, Frank noticed as he fought to hold on to the bucking hose. The loggers were so organized, he had a feeling they'd been through all this before.

"They found someone!" Callie shouted just then. "Look! They're bringing him out now!"

The volunteers surged forward as three men emerged from the flaming mill carrying a blanket-covered body. Frank heard another siren over the noise of the crowd and swiveled around to see an ambulance arriving.

Almost instantly a pair of paramedics worked their way through the crowd with a stretcher and a portable oxygen tank. Frank strained to see who the victim was, but smoke and the crowd blocked his view. He knew Callie was even more anxious than he was.

Fifteen minutes later the paramedics passed through the crowd on their way back to their ambulance, this time carrying the body of a huge man, now completely covered with the blanket.

"It's Buster!" Frank heard everyone murmur as the stretcher passed by them. "Buster Owens! Burned in his own mill!"

"Oh, no." Frank turned to Callie. Her face revealed a mixture of horror at Owens's death and relief that it wasn't her uncle. Suddenly she began to cry. Frank put an arm around her.

"He must have died from smoke inhalation," Joe shouted to them, dazed. "I wonder what started the fire?"

Before anyone could answer, they were interrupted by Stan Shaw. "Callie!" he was shouting as he jogged toward them from the parking lot. "Are you okay?"

"Uncle Stan!" Callie broke free from Frank to run to hug her uncle. Stan Shaw looked perfectly fine, though he was obviously stunned and confused by all that was going on.

"I don't believe it," Stan said when Callie told him what had happened. "I was talking with Buster less than an hour ago. Poor guy."

Just then, another explosion sounded from the mill. Glass from several windows was blown out, and a few of the people near the front of the crowd cried out as shards dug into their skin.

"They've been cut!" someone shouted. "Stop the ambulance!"

The ambulance carrying Buster Owens had already disappeared up the road, though.

"Stan Shaw!" Freddy Zackarias, the skinny, loud-mouthed logger from the general store, shouted. "You've got a first-aid kit in your truck, don't you?"

"Right!" Stan turned to the teenagers. "Come on! I have some blankets, too. Let someone else take over that hose."

Frank, Joe, and Callie quickly transferred the hose to waiting hands and followed Stan at a fast jog to his truck on the edge of the lot.

"Hey, Stan," Frank called as he caught up with the older man. "I meant to ask you something. We saw your truck here earlier. What were you—"

"Yes?" Stan's hand froze as he opened the back of the truck. "What was I what, Frank?"

Frank leaned into the truck to pull blankets out. "What were you doing here? We thought maybe Buster Owens was—" Frank's words died on his lips. The blanket he was holding had been partially concealing something.

Frank stared at what had been hidden beneath the blankets. There, beside a first-aid kit, was an open crate. In the crate lay more than a dozen sticks of dynamite!

Chapter

3

"WHAT'S UP?" Joe asked, reaching past his brother for the first-aid kit. When he saw what was inside he gasped out loud.

"Excuse me, Stan. What are you doing with a truck full of dynamite?"

"A what?" Callie demanded, peering around Frank and Joe. As she saw the dynamite and took in the situation her mouth dropped open. "Uncle Stan," she said in a deadly calm voice, "what's that doing there?"

"I don't know," her uncle said, sweat forming on his forehead. "I've never seen it before. I swear!"

"Your truck was here earlier," Joe said quietly, almost as though talking to himself. "We saw it. After the explosion we noticed it was gone."

22

He was interrupted by the screech of a walkie-talkie, and spun around to see a sheriff approaching with a radio in his hand.

"Uh, Sheriff F-Ferris!" Stan stammered, turning his back on the truck. "Can I help you?"

"You sure can, Stan," the sheriff said, nodding briefly to Callie and the boys. "I heard you have some first-aid supplies we can use. My deputy took my kit out and forgot to replace it. They've got all the injured folks laid out in the parking lot right now, but the nearest ambulance is thirty miles away. Looks like we're going to have to fix 'em up ourselves."

"Right. Uh, you know my niece, Callie." As Joe watched, Stan pulled Callie in front of him and used her almost as a shield. "And these two boys are friends of hers from back East. Frank and Joe Hardy—their dad's a detective!"

"Pleased to meet you," the sheriff said hurriedly, touching his hat to the Hardys. He hesitated midgesture. "Your dad's not Fenton Hardy, is he? The guy who solved that big show-business case down in Los Angeles a few years back?"

"Yes, sir," Joe said.

"Well, well! It's a shame he's not here now to help investigate this catastrophe," the sheriff said. "There must be half a million dollars' worth of damage here so far, and that's just to the buildings alone. We can thank our stars the place was closed today."

He pulled out a handkerchief and mopped his

brow. When he took it down it was black from soot and sweat. "I'd better get those supplies. You don't mind, do you?" he asked Stan as he edged past him to the truck.

Stan, Callie, and the Hardys watched helplessly as the sheriff leaned inside.

He froze. Behind him, Stan coughed.

"Stan," the sheriff said gravely, straightening up. "What's this dynamite doing in here?"

"I—I—I don't know, Sheriff. I've never seen it b-before," Stan stammered, turning pale.

"Someone must have planted it on him," Callie defended her uncle. "They're trying to get him blamed for this fire."

The sheriff stepped away from the car, all of a sudden very professional and serious. "There are half a dozen sticks missing. Why?"

"He told you he doesn't know!" Joe broke in. "Anyway, you don't know that the fire was started by dynamite, do you?"

The sheriff shook his head. "I radioed the county seat for a couple of fire investigators. I admit I don't know much about fires, but I do know that this got started too fast and too loud to be anything natural. My guess is that an explosive of some kind had to be used. Also, the longer this mill's closed, the longer your trees stay up, right, Stan?"

Joe turned to Stan, wondering why he didn't speak up in his own defense. The conservationist had turned an unhealthy shade of gray and seemed to be too stunned to speak.

"How about if my brother and I take the first-aid supplies to the volunteers while you talk to Mr. Shaw?" Frank said, breaking the awkward silence.

"Good idea," the sheriff said, shooing them away.

"I'm staying," Callie insisted. "I know my uncle Stan couldn't have had anything to do with this."

"Fine." Joe lifted the heavy first-aid kit out while Frank grabbed some blankets. "We'll be back in a few minutes."

As soon as they were out of earshot, Joe said to his brother, "Okay, what gives? You were so eager to get away from there I could practically smell the rubber burning on your hiking boots."

"I might be wrong," Frank said as they hurried toward the group of injured people, "but Stan Shaw seems like a straightforward guy to me. If he says he doesn't know how that dynamite got in his truck, he doesn't. That means somebody planted it on him."

"But why didn't he even try to defend himself?" Joe asked. "He practically surrendered to the sheriff before the guy even suspected anything!"

"He must have panicked," Frank replied. "I mean, think about it. You live in a town where no one really likes you, and you're caught at an explosion with a bunch of dynamite. He must already be figuring how he'll come up with bail."

"But if he didn't do it—" Joe said.

25

"Whoever *did* planted that dynamite in the last half hour," Frank interrupted. "Now the faster we start tracking down who did it, the better our chances are."

"But who *would* do a thing like that?" Joe demanded. "Were they out to get Buster, or did he just happen to get caught in the blast?"

"Finding that out," Frank answered, "is how we pay for those pancakes you ate. Here's the first-aid kit you asked for," Frank said to a volunteer standing with the injured. "We have blankets, too. Is there anything else you want or need?"

"We didn't ask for anything." A busy woman glanced up from where she was bandaging a young man's arm. "We used the supplies from the fire truck. I think everybody's just about taken care of now."

"But the sheriff said . . ." Joe's voice trailed off. He was puzzled.

"If anyone shows up with a case of soda, though, you can bring that right on over," the woman joked, turning back to her patient.

"Frank, what's that all about?" Joe asked as soon as the brothers had moved a short distance from the crowd. "Someone asked us *and* the sheriff for first-aid supplies nobody needed?"

"Yeah, somebody who wanted that dynamite to be found in Stan's truck," Frank replied. "I'll bet it was the same somebody who planted it there."

"So you think someone's trying to frame Stan for this fire—and for Owens's murder?"

"It's all I can think if we believe Stan's innocent," Frank answered. "What we've got to find out, though, is what Stan was doing here before the explosion. He sure acted as if he was hiding something. Maybe whatever it is has something to do with why that dynamite turned up in his truck."

Joe had to stop to cough to clear some of the smoke from his lungs. Then he took off at a jog to catch up with his brother, who was heading back to Stan. As they approached the truck, Joe saw he wouldn't be able to question Stan in private. The sheriff was still with him.

"I'm sorry, Stan," the sheriff was saying as Joe and Frank joined them. "I've known you for almost ten years, but the law's the law. This truck has to be impounded so I can thoroughly search it, and you're going to have to come in for questioning."

"My uncle's not a criminal!" Callie exploded, pulling away from Frank, who was holding her to calm her down. "He was here about an hour ago. We all saw his truck. That must have been when somebody planted the dynamite in his truck. Stan couldn't have anything to do with it!"

The sheriff turned to Stan, who took a quick hop-step backward. "You were here earlier, Stan?" the sheriff demanded. "Before the explosion?"

"Well, sure, I—I—" Stan stammered. He glanced at Callie, who clapped a hand over her mouth as she realized what she'd said. "I was just—"

"Don't say any more." The sheriff took him by the arm and steered him toward the patrol car. "You can tell me the rest in my office—where I can read you your rights and we can get it all recorded. I think you'd better call a lawyer when we get back," he added as the two men walked away.

Callie, Joe, and Frank stared after the sheriff and Stan. Joe noticed that Stan didn't even glance back at them. It was as though he felt guilty.

Joe was lost in his thoughts and didn't hear the tall, athletic-looking young woman in khaki pants and T-shirt striding up to them. Her hair was long and blond and pulled back into a ponytail that was covered with oily soot from the fire.

"Ronnie," Callie was saying, "you won't believe what happened. This is my boyfriend, Frank Hardy, and his brother, Joe," she added hastily. To the Hardys she explained, "Ronnie Croft owns and edits Crosscut's weekly newspaper."

"The Crosscut *Guardian*," Ronnie said proudly, shaking the Hardys' hands. "What could possibly have happened that hasn't already gone on today?" she demanded of Callie.

As Callie told her about her uncle Stan's arrest, Ronnie's jaw dropped. "I'm going to the station," she said. "You want to come along?"

"Definitely," Callie said. "Uncle Stan seems to be in shock about all this. I want to be there to help if I can. What about you?" she asked Frank and Joe.

"We'll hang around here a little longer," Frank said calmly. "We'll meet you at the sheriff's later, if that's okay."

"If I'm not there I'll be at the newspaper office," Callie agreed as she started off with Ronnie toward the newswoman's car. "Boy, am I glad you guys came with me this summer. I didn't know how much I'd need you."

"Hear that, Frank?" Joe couldn't resist teasing as Callie and Ronnie walked away. "She needs you. A mystery to solve *and* a girlfriend who needs you. What more can a guy ask for in a day?"

"Answers, for a start," Frank said with a frown. "Let's head out to where we saw Buster's truck pulled off the road. I want to see if it's still there, and if we can tell anything from it. But first we should pick up our packs. My camera's in mine, and we might need it."

"Right, boss." Joe took off after his older brother. "Then we can catch a ride back to town for lunch. It's way past noon, and I'm starved."

Most of the onlookers were leaving now that the fire was in the smoldering stage. The fire fighters had to stay to douse any flare-ups.

"Hey, Joe," Frank said. "Look over there."

Joe followed Frank's gaze to a cluster of loggers standing next to a battered station wagon, talking in the far corner of the lot. He recognized several of them from the general store that morning. Mike Stavisky was easy to recognize, with his muscular build and heavy black beard. Skinny Freddy Zackarias stood beside him, nodding at everything Mike said.

"Let's wander by there," Frank said softly. "I want to hear what they're saying."

It didn't take long for Stan's name to come up in the conversation. "There was dynamite in Stan's truck," he heard Mike tell the others. "He must have heard that the Forest Service was going to let Horizon cut down his precious redwoods after all. Him and his assistant have been causing trouble around here for years. I knew sooner or later one of 'em would pull something like this."

"But Stan Shaw?" a short, baby-faced logger interrupted. "If it was Galen I'd understand. He's threatened to blow up every mill in the state. But Stan's kinda reasonable for a tree hugger."

"There's no such thing as a reasonable tree hugger!" Mike boomed. "What's bad for logging is bad for your wallet, Nat, and don't you forget it. Stan lost his patience, that's all, and now he's going to pay for it."

"What's *his* problem?" Joe whispered to Frank as the brothers moved away before they got spotted.

"He probably believes what he's saying, but he's not making things any easier for anybody,"

Frank replied grimly. "The trouble is, the others are listening to him. Let's hurry up and get those packs. I want to get a look at Buster's truck."

"I'm not up to walking across those logs just now. What do you say we jog down to the bridge," Joe said.

The packs were right where they had left them. They shouldered theirs, and Frank carried Callie's as they made their way back across the bridge and along the riverbank toward the abandoned truck.

"There it is," Joe said after a short while, pointing through the trees. Where there was no mud the red paint gleamed in the afternoon sun. It was parked in the same spot where Callie and the boys had spotted it earlier. "It's at kind of a weird angle. Do you think Buster could have been forced off the road?"

"I don't know, but don't touch anything," Frank reminded him. "If Sheriff Ferris is such a by-the-book cop, we don't want to mess up any evidence for him."

"Don't worry," Joe replied. "I'll be sure and— Hey, look," he said, stopping abruptly near the driver's side. He pointed to the trampled muddy ground around the driver's door. "It looks like there was some kind of struggle here," he said. "See the tracks?"

Frank appeared beside him, inspecting the mess of footprints. "Men's feet, definitely. Look how big the prints are," he said. "It looks like they were wearing boots."

"Those hobnailed boots the loggers wear?" Joe ventured excitedly.

Frank nodded. "Maybe. It sure was good it rained last night."

As Frank knelt down to inspect the footprints more closely, Joe's gaze swung down the length of the truck. His eyes caught on a flash of bright lime green color a short distance away. "What's that?" he asked, walking toward the bushes.

"What?" Frank asked.

"It's a cap. Buster was wearing a cap just like this." Joe whipped out a handkerchief and picked the duck-billed cap off the bush. It had the orange-and-purple Horizon Lumber insignia on it.

"Yep, I bet this is it," he called to Frank as he walked back to join his brother. "Oh, wow. It's stained or something—" Joe stopped dead in his tracks.

"What's the matter?" Frank asked, staring at him.

Joe held up the cap and slowly turned it to show his brother. "Blood!" was all he said.

Chapter

4

"LET ME SEE THAT." Frank reached for the cap. He took it, holding on to the handkerchief, and examined it more closely. The entire back of the lime-colored cap was dark with blood.

"Whoever wore this could have been slugged hard from behind," Frank remarked.

"There's a black hair here on the inside," said Joe. "Buster had black hair, right? This is his truck, so it's probably his cap, too."

"Or his attacker's," Frank pointed out. "Several guys were wearing these at the general store and at the fire." He handed the cap back to Joe and put down his pack. "I'm going to take some pictures of these footprints," he said. "There are a couple of clear impressions here. The sheriff might be able to use them."

"Let's just hope they're not Stan's," Joe said, and wandered off to search for more clues.

33

Frank had snapped half a dozen shots when he heard his brother cry out again. "Hey, Frank! Look over here!"

Frank joined his brother a short distance down the logging road. At Joe's feet was a different set of tire marks. From their depth it looked as if the vehicle had pulled out in a hurry.

"That's not all," Joe said. "Look at that."

Frank squatted down to inspect the ground surrounding the tire tracks. A pair of furrows were cut into the mud, flanked by a single bootprint on either side. "It looks like someone dragged something to the truck," he said slowly, "and probably loaded it into the vehicle here."

"What if it was a body they were dragging?" Joe asked, examining the furrows. "These marks could be made by the heels of someone's shoes. Someone could have loaded Buster into a car, driven back to the mill, then dumped his body in the main building. Then the guy set a few sticks of dynamite on fire with a long fuse."

"You think Buster was already dead when the explosion was set?" Frank asked.

"What difference does it make? Dead or just out cold, he wouldn't have a chance to save himself." Joe shook his head in disgust. "This is murder, Frank. I have a real gut feeling about it."

"I'm with you," Frank admitted. "But if we're right, the question is, why? I don't care how weird Stan was acting, he's not about to start murdering loggers. There have got to be

34

other people who had grudges against Buster Owens—after all, he owned a mill and had to hire and fire people.

"We really don't know enough yet to make a list of suspects," Frank continued. "We'd better take this evidence to the sheriff. Maybe it'll help spring Stan, at least. But first let me finish my roll of film on these bootprints. This one over here is almost perfect."

"I'll take care of the hat." Joe produced a plastic bag from his backpack. "It can't hurt to keep any possible fingerprints clean."

"I'll tell you what," Frank said. "If the sheriff says you did a good job with the evidence, I'll buy you lunch."

"Yeah, right." Joe followed Frank onto the logging road. "It'll be dinnertime by the time we get back to town. Lunch won't even be a possibility."

Frank and Joe decided to go back to the mill to catch a ride into town. When they got there the fire appeared to be completely out. All that remained of the morning's crowd were a couple of fire fighters casually hosing down the jagged, black rubble—the remains of Horizon Lumber. Frank spotted two men in suits leaving the ruins for the parking lot. "Those must be the fire investigators the sheriff called," he said.

"Maybe we can hitch a ride with them," Joe replied.

The boys approached the edge of the burned

central building where the strangers had stopped to talk to the two fire fighters. "There are still hot spots in there that want to burst into flames," Frank heard the taller of the two tell the volunteers. "The only way to make sure it's dead is to keep hosing it down."

The fire fighters agreed, and the investigators continued on toward the parking lot. As they stopped beside a car with an emblem on the door, Frank and Joe ran up to them.

"Excuse me, sir?" Frank caught up with the taller man just as he was opening the car door. "My name's Frank Hardy and this is my brother, Joe. We were helping fight the fire and seem to have missed our ride back to town. We were wondering if we could catch a ride with you."

"Sure, Frank," said the tall man as he dusted some ash off his pants. "I'm Jerry, and this is my partner, Ollie. If you boys helped fight this you earned a ride. But we have to hurry. We need to get a package ready for the state crime lab as soon as we can."

Frank and Joe climbed in the backseat as the two men got into the front.

As the car headed back for town, Frank spoke up. "Are you the guys sent to investigate the building?" They both nodded. "Did you find out how the fire started?"

"Well, we're not supposed to talk about it, but I guess you deserve an answer or two," Jerry said, glancing amiably at Frank in the rearview mirror. "Unfortunately, the answer is yes *and* no. We found out where the fire started—close to a tangle of hydraulic lines by one of the big saws—and we could see that it spread fast, real fast. What we don't know yet is what caused it, and that's what the lab's going to tell us."

"How?" asked Joe.

"Easy," Ollie replied. His voice was a husky bass that sounded as if all his high notes had been burned out. "You may not know this, but explosives manufacturers are required to include microscopic amounts of certain materials in their products. That means every explosive leaves behind a signature. All we have to do is scrape up some of the debris, analyze it for specific elements, and—ta-dah—we got you. If you ask me, we're going to find some explosives here. The hoses weren't worn out. They were blown off the rigging. And that spells explosives to me."

Frank glanced at his brother. The chances seemed excellent that the debris would match the dynamite in Stan's truck. That might be all the evidence the sheriff needed to file charges against the environmentalist.

"How long does it take to get the lab results back?" he asked Ollie, trying to sound calm.

"Four to five days, usually," Ollie replied. "We'll put a rush on this one, though, since there may be a murder involved. We should hear from the lab in seventy-two hours, max." Ollie turned toward Frank and Joe. "Why are you boys so curious?"

"No reason," Frank said lamely. He stared out the window and saw the town of Crosscut swing into view. "We can get out here," he told Jerry. "Thanks again for the ride."

"Anytime." Jerry stopped the car to let the boys out. "Don't play with matches now, hear?"

"What's that supposed to mean?" Joe asked, annoyed, as the brothers crossed the street toward the sheriff's office.

"I think it means quit asking questions because it makes us look suspicious," Frank replied. He eyed the modern exterior of the sheriff's office, set at the opposite end of Main Street from the general store. "If that's the case, Sheriff Ferris is going to be enormously suspicious in about five minutes," he added as they walked through the door.

Sheriff Ferris's desk was just inside the entrance. When Frank and Joe entered, the sheriff was talking quietly into the phone. A look of impatience flickered across his face when he saw the Hardys. He placed a hand over the mouthpiece. "May I help you boys?" he said. "I'm kind of busy right now."

"We have something you might be interested in," Joe said, holding up the plastic bag with the bloodstained cap inside. "We found Buster Owens's truck about a quarter mile from the mill. This was near it. We think he might have been in some kind of struggle."

Sheriff Ferris said something into the phone and hung up. Then he motioned the boys to sit down. "What makes you think that?" he asked brusquely as the boys removed their backpacks.

Joe set the bag with the cap on Ferris's desk. "It's bloodstained," he said. "We think it's Buster's."

"You moved a piece of evidence?" Ferris said angrily. "Don't you boys know I could have you arrested for that?"

Frank cleared his throat. "We wanted you to see this as soon as possible, because if that is Buster's blood, then he didn't just *happen* to be in his mill when it exploded. He could have been murdered. And, while you may think Stan Shaw started that fire, we think the real murderer may be getting away."

"Oh, so you're sure it couldn't be Callie's uncle." Sheriff Ferris shook his head. "Look, boys," he said finally. "I know your father's a famous detective. But Crosscut is my town, and I'd appreciate it if you didn't mess around with my crime scenes. The job's tough enough as it is. You got that?"

Frank held his gaze steadily for a moment. Then he said reluctantly, "Yes, sir. But I think you should know, there were some prints around the truck. It looked like there'd been a scuffle, and one guy apparently dragged the other a short distance to another car. I took pictures of the prints in case you needed them."

"Then hand them over!" the sheriff snapped.

"I'd prefer to develop them myself," Frank said calmly. "Also, Joe and I would like to see Stan Shaw."

The sheriff stared at Frank in amazement, but finally he laughed. "All right, you win," he said. "I'll go check out the truck. You get me those prints by the end of the day. Eight by tens, understand? Stan is in a holding cell at the end of the hall. Ronnie Croft and Callie are with him."

Frank and Joe thanked the sheriff, picked up the backpacks, and headed toward the holding pens. "Not bad, Frank," Joe commented as they opened a heavy door with a wire-covered window. "I was sure we were going to get arrested in there."

"You just have to know how to talk to people, Joe," Frank said with a grin as they entered a room with a central hallway leading past a couple of empty cells. At the end of the hall stood Callie and Ronnie. They were talking to Stan, who was standing with his shoulders slumped forward and his head hanging, in the last cell.

"Frank!" Callie said. "We thought you'd never get here. Did you find out anything?"

"A little," Frank said with a nod to Ronnie and Stan. "Have you been charged with anything?" Frank asked Stan.

"Not yet," Callie answered for her uncle. "The sheriff has just questioned him. We don't think Ferris has enough evidence to make any formal charges. But someone from Save the Redwoods headquarters is on his way here to help out if necessary. Now, what about you?''

Frank and Joe brought the others up to date on what they had found on the mountain. Callie, Stan, and Ronnie reacted with surprise and shock. "Who would purposely murder Buster Owens?" Stan blurted out when Frank had finished. "Everyone in town liked Buster."

"I hate to say it, but right now you're the only suspect, Stan," Frank advised him.

"We'll do anything we can to help prove your innocence, but we'll need a lot more information—especially from you—first," Joe explained.

Stan nodded. "I know. Callie's told me what good detectives you two are." He grinned wearily. "What do you need to know?"

"Is there any way you would profit from Buster's death?" Frank asked bluntly.

Stan's eyes widened. "Just the opposite," he replied simply. "Buster and I were just starting to make progress on an agreement concerning some timberlands around Crosscut. It was important to me, because Buster had been so stubborn about conservation for years."

"Who else knew about the agreement?" Joe asked.

Stan thought for a moment. "Walter Ecks, Buster's foreman, knew. And maybe Millie, Buster's daughter. Buster wanted to keep it as hush-hush as possible until he got all the details worked out."

Frank nodded. "At least there are one or two

witnesses," he said. "They can help prove you had no motive to kill Owens. Just one more question. What was your meeting with Buster about this afternoon?"

Stan drew back as though Frank had slapped him. "The meeting? That—that was a personal matter. It had nothing to do with what happened later. It's nothing that concerns you."

"It would help, though, if we knew more," Joe emphasized, watching him.

Stan shook his head. "No. I swore I wouldn't discuss it. Buster's dead now, and I don't believe I should—" Unexpectedly, Stan's eyes teared up.

Frank glanced at Callie and cleared his throat. "Uh, we have some photographs to develop here," he said briskly. "Is there a darkroom in town?"

"There's one at the newspaper," Ronnie Croft volunteered. "If it'll help Stan, it's all yours. Are you guys hungry?" Frank and Joe nodded. "I'll order some sandwiches from the Potbelly and you can eat before you work. Okay?"

"I'll stay here with Uncle Stan," Callie said. "You guys go ahead."

The offices of the Crosscut *Guardian* were small but cozy, Frank discovered—tucked into a storefront on Main Street near the Potbelly Café. "Not a bad operation," he commented as he inspected Ronnie's printing equipment, police scanner, computer, piles of paper, and other signs of an active and successful community newspaper. "It must be fun, running a paper, with no boss to tell you what to do."

"Yeah, I like it," Ronnie admitted, opening the door of a converted closet to show the Hardys her tiny darkroom. "Of course, when the fights over forest land get going I have to be careful to stay neutral. Otherwise," she added with a grimace, "I'm likely to lose half my subscribers. Oh well, I guess you can't please everybody."

Half an hour later the sandwiches were eaten, and Ronnie had started writing about the fire on her computer. As Frank and Joe were pouring chemicals into developing trays, they heard a commotion outside the darkroom. Frank stuck his head out of the room to see Ronnie standing at the front window, peering out at a mob scene in the street.

"What's going on?" Frank asked, stepping out of the darkroom. Joe followed him.

"A bunch of loggers are chasing Vance Galen down the street." Ronnie was very tense. "They're throwing things at him. They must think he's responsible for Buster's death."

"Come on. We'd better help him," Joe said.

"No need to hurry," Ronnie said grimly. "He's heading straight here."

Just then the door flew open and Galen ran in. He slammed the door behind him and leaned against it, panting. "Wow!" he shouted, wild-eyed. "Did you see that? I thought they were going to kill me! They're saying I burned Buster's mill down!"

Ronnie stared at him with obvious distaste. "Well," she said, "*did* you?"

"Of course not!" Galen sputtered, glaring first at her, then at the Hardys. "And I didn't kill Buster Owens either, if that's what you're thinking. Not that I hadn't considered the idea more than once."

Frank stared out the window. Half a dozen men were standing in the street outside the newspaper, yelling threats at Galen. Frank recognized Mike Stavisky among them. A man he hadn't seen before—hawk-nosed, with a receding hairline and a muscular build—hung back from the rest of the crowd, watching calmly.

"They definitely believe you did more than consider it," Frank remarked to Galen. "What do they think—that you and Stan were accomplices?"

"Stan?" Galen stared at him, not comprehending. "What's he got to do with this?"

"He's in jail, Vance," Ronnie said acidly. "They found a crate of dynamite in his truck and now the sheriff's holding him for questioning. Where have you been?"

"Stan? I can't believe it!" Galen's expression was a combination of shock and relief. "It's a good thing they didn't find it in my car," he added, half to himself. "They'd probably have hanged me by now."

Frank could see that the loggers outside were growing impatient. "Vance Galen, come out here!" Stavisky yelled. "We want an explanation about where you were today!"

The other loggers roared their assent. Ronnie turned to Galen. "Go on," she said dryly. "Tell them where you were this morning—if you can."

Frank looked at Ronnie. Clearly, she had no sympathy for the overly dramatic Green. But did she think Galen really was capable of murdering Buster Owens?

"No way I'm going out there," Galen said. "I'm staying put until they get bored and go away."

Before Ronnie could object, Galen ducked behind the massive press. Frank shook his head, then turned his attention back to the loggers. With Stavisky urging them on, they were getting angrier by the second. "They're not going—" Frank started to say.

He was cut off by a loud crash that filled the office. The front plate-glass window had shattered into a thousand pieces!

FRANK INSTINCTIVELY LEAPT to one side, and the big shards of glass missed him by just inches. Joe had dived behind a stack of newspapers, but Ronnie hadn't taken cover at all. She was striding forward, red-faced, toward the window.

"Mike Stavisky!" she yelled. "You broke my window! I'm calling Sheriff Ferris!"

"Sorry, Ronnie." Stavisky's sheepish face appeared in the jagged opening made by the rock. "I got carried away—"

"I know you did!" Ronnie glared at him. "Who's going to pay for the damage?"

"We will, Ronnie."

Frank stood up in time to see one of the other loggers, a tall, thin man with an embarrassed expression, join Stavisky. "We didn't mean to break the window," he tried to explain. "It's just a lot of us lost our jobs because of that fire. Also Buster, who was a friend and a good boss. And then Galen—"

"Vance Galen is innocent until proven guilty, just like every one of you," Ronnie said evenly as Frank and Joe joined her on either side. "And so is Stan Shaw, for that matter. We've had enough trouble in this town, haven't we? Let's not start it up again."

"You're right," the tall logger said, though he looked more disgusted than convinced. Then he turned to the others in the group. Frank noticed that the hawk-nosed man in the back had disappeared.

"Go on, guys," the tall logger said. "Mike and I will get some boards and cover this window until we can get a new one cut."

"We'll what?" Mike gaped at his friend.

"You heard him," Ronnie said to Stavisky. "And while you're at it, you'll let Galen get out of here—in one piece."

The loggers obeyed Ronnie grudgingly. While Frank watched, amazed, Vance Galen stood up from behind the printing press and ventured outside. He skitted off down the middle of the road like a gunman in the Old West expecting gunfire at any minute.

"I never did like that man," Ronnie mused, turning her back on the street. "Well, I'm going to get a broom. I guess you two want to get back to the darkroom."

"Congratulations," Joe said as the Hardys headed toward their closet. "That was quick work."

Ronnie blushed. "Oh, those guys don't scare me," she said. "I grew up with most of 'em. I've been bossing them around since elementary school."

"Who was that guy standing at the back of the crowd?" Frank asked. "The older one with the receding hairline and the hawk nose? He didn't seem to belong with the others."

"That's Rafe Collins," Ronnie said. "He's the foreman at Johnson Lumber, and not a nice guy at all, if you ask me. I hear he really knocks heads together if the loggers don't make their quotas by the end of the month. That's how the company stays successful, though—or so Johnson says, anyway."

"I wonder what he was doing with that mob," Frank said.

Ronnie paused. "Well, for one thing, Johnson and Galen hate each other's guts," she told Frank. "Galen thinks Johnson's guilty of greed, mismanaging the environment, killing off endangered species, and all kinds of other evils. And Johnson honestly believes the Greens want to put him out of business. Collins probably wanted to find out what happened to Galen so he could report to Johnson later."

She sighed as she hunted up the broom in a corner closet. "I tell you, if it weren't for Stan

Shaw, this town would have blown up years ago."

Less than an hour later Joe watched as Frank pulled the last of the second set of photographs from the shallow developing tray and hung them on a photo clamp to drain. Turning to Joe, he said, "Let's take the first set over to the sheriff. While he's looking them over, we can try to pry out of him anything he's uncovered."

"Good idea." Joe gathered up the set of photographs from the stack beside the print dryer. "Callie should still be there."

The Hardys said goodbye to Ronnie, who was supervising the loggers' window repair job, and headed out into the twilight for the sheriff's office. Main Street was empty, but Joe could hear music and laughter coming from the Potbelly Café and saw lights glowing in the Sportsman's Pool Hall.

At the far end of the three-block town, the sheriff's office blazed with lights as well. Several vehicles bearing the logos of various state and county law enforcement agencies had pulled up close to the front door.

"Looks like the sheriff is going to be up late tonight," Frank remarked as they entered the office.

The boys had to wait only five minutes before being ushered into a back office despite the confusion of a constantly ringing telephone and several uniformed people in conference in the front room.

"All right, boys," Ferris said as Frank and Joe sat down facing the desk. "What have you got for me?"

Joe handed Ferris the photographs while Frank said, "In some of the pictures you can see a bootprint clearly enough to tell it's from a typical logger's hobnailed boot. It's a good thing there was rain last night."

Ferris squared the stack of photos on his desk, then cleared his throat. "Thanks. These will help with our investigation. But I don't think—"

As soon as Joe sensed the sheriff was giving them the brush-off, he jumped in with a question. "Has anyone tested the blood on the cap we found yet, sir?" he asked.

Ferris turned to Joe with narrowed eyes. "I ordered a test. The results will be back tomorrow. The coroner called me, though. The autopsy's not complete yet, but he did confirm that Buster had a serious head injury before he died in the fire."

"Was he robbed?" Joe asked, eager to keep Ferris talking.

"Nope," Ferris replied. He pulled a large plastic bag from the desk drawer. Joe saw that it contained a worn leather wallet, a pocketknife, and a half-empty pack of gum.

"These are his things," Ferris said. "There was over two hundred dollars in his wallet, so I guess we can rule out robbery as a motive."

"But it was definitely murder," Joe said. "Buster didn't just happen to be in the mill when it exploded. He was dumped there."

Ferris's lips twitched irritably. "I'd appreciate it if you'd keep me posted on anything else you turn up while you're here."

Frank stood up, reaching out to shake Ferris's hand. "Is Callie still here?"

"She left an hour ago," he answered gruffly. "One of those Green fellows showed up from headquarters. She said to tell you they were going to pick up your rental car from Stan's place and bring it down here for you. They'll meet you back at the cabin later on."

"Mind if we see Stan?" Frank asked.

"Sorry. Visiting hours are over. He'll be here tomorrow morning. Now, if you'll excuse me, I've got a lot of details to attend to."

"Some attitude he has," Joe muttered to his brother as they left the building. "He wants all the information we can give him, as long as we stay officially outside the investigation."

"It makes sense," Frank said. "Look at all the other professionals crawling around this place. Ferris wants to impress them."

"Well, we don't have anyone to impress, so maybe we'll work faster," Joe remarked, gazing down the short street. "Did anything about Owens's belongings in that bag strike you as weird, Frank? I mean, like something was missing?"

Frank thought for a moment. "Nothing that I

can think of. I only saw the man once, though. What did you have in mind?"

"Nothing, really." Joe frowned. "Just a feeling . . . How about grabbing a snack before we meet up with Callie?" he suggested, heading toward the pool hall, which sported a small neon sign that read Good Eats. "Maybe we can pick up some gossip inside."

"Good idea," Frank agreed. "We can call Callie from there."

The Sportsman's Pool Hall was like an old-fashioned hunting lodge, Joe realized as he and Frank entered the large, square room. Stuffed deer, bear, and moose heads studded the rustic wooden walls, and a smoky haze hung over the three pool tables and collection of tables. While Joe sat down at one of the tables and ordered stew and biscuits for two, Frank went off in search of a phone booth to make a call to Callie.

Joe watched along with a few local people as two men shot some pool. They were talking about the day's tragedy, and didn't seem to notice that Joe was taking in every word they said.

"What I want to know is, who's going to take over Horizon Lumber," said the short, bow-legged man with a curly brown beard.

His tall, hefty companion frowned as he aimed at the cue ball. "Buster's daughter, Millie, most likely. She always wanted to run the place, but her dad wouldn't let her. They used to fight about it all the time."

"You think she'll pay us while they rebuild the mill?" asked the first man.

"I doubt it. Why should she?" his friend replied. "I don't know what we're going to do. I heard Johnson's not hiring."

"What'd you hear?" Frank took a seat next to Joe and spoke in a low voice. "Do they know anything we don't?"

Joe waited until the waitress had served their food. Then, as they ate, he told his brother, "They think Buster's daughter is going to run the mill. They say she and her dad used to fight a lot." His expression darkened as an idea came to him. "Do you think she could have had anything to do with his death?"

Frank frowned. "It seems unlikely. I doubt that the average female could have knocked a three-hundred-pound man over the head and dragged him into a car by herself. And remember, those footprints by the truck were all really big. Besides, she's his daughter—she'd stand to inherit the mill eventually anyway. Why wouldn't she just wait?"

He chewed thoughtfully for a moment. "Still, it wouldn't hurt to check her out," he added.

"I still think there's something about that bag of Owens's belongings," Joe said, annoyed with himself. "I can't put my finger on it, though."

"Don't worry about it," said Frank. "It'll come to you sooner or later. By the way, Callie begged us to go rescue her from that Save the

Redwoods guy. It seems he's a real jerk—he's asking her so many questions about how Stan got into this mess that she wants to commit murder herself. I say we finish our stew and head up to Stan's right away."

It was fully dark by the time Frank and Joe stepped outside the Sportsman's Pool Hall. The street was deserted. A full moon had just topped the mountain in back of town, casting the road in a silvery light. Joe's gaze ran down the row of cars parked along Main Street until he spotted their rented jeep. Parked next to it was a flatbed truck loaded with several huge logs. It had a Horizon Lumber logo on its side.

"There it is," Joe announced, leading the way. When he reached the jeep, he poked his head inside and added, "The key's in the ignition."

"What an amazing place," Frank commented as he walked around to the passenger door. "Someone commits murder in broad daylight, but people still leave the keys in their cars."

"Good thing the rental agent insisted we get four-wheel drive," Joe commented to his brother. "That mountain road up to Stan's is going to be slippery."

"They probably don't rent anything else to people headed this way," Frank said. He opened the door of the jeep, but then hesitated.

"Did you hear that?" he asked Joe.

"What?"

Joe listened. In the silence he heard a loud,

metallic *pop*. Then, to his surprise, an ear-splitting screech followed, and after that an ominous rumble.

"Frank!" Joe cried, his eyes wide as he stared at the logging truck behind his brother. "Watch out! Those logs—they're falling!"

Chapter

6

FRANK AND JOE dove for cover—Frank beneath the flatbed truck itself and Joe beneath the car behind the rented jeep. An instant later Frank heard the first of the enormous logs crash onto the ground where he'd been standing. He glanced to his right in time to spot a pair of hobnailed boots land in the street and sprint away.

"Joe, are you okay?" Frank shouted as two more logs rolled off the truck, causing a noise like thunder. The door of the pool hall had swung open and half a dozen customers came out.

Joe's answer was a long time coming. When the logs finally stopped rolling, Frank heard him say shakily, "That was no accident. Let's get that guy!"

Joe must have seen him, too, Frank realized,

rolling out from under the truck and rising to a crouch as he inspected the storefronts along Main Street.

There were a lot of people on the street now, and it would be impossible to identify their attacker. "Forget it, Joe," Frank said, his voice thick with disappointment.

"I guess you're right," Joe said, joining him. "But we can look in the truck. The creep split so fast he might have left something behind to identify him."

"You check the flatbed," Frank agreed. "I'll explain to the people on the street what happened."

Five minutes later, after Frank asked someone to call the sheriff about the fallen logs, he returned to the truck and called to Joe. "Find anything yet?" he asked.

"You bet." Joe emerged from the cab holding a large set of bolt cutters and a pair of work gloves. "These were on the flatbed," Joe explained. "They're probably what he used to break the chain. I guess the gloves mean there won't be any fingerprints. There's an open toolbox in the back of the cab, so I guess he stole them from there."

"Unless the guy was a Horizon employee and the toolbox was his," Frank pointed out grimly.

"But why go after us?" Joe protested. "Did someone see us hanging around Buster's truck? Are they trying to keep us from investigating Buster's murder?"

Frank shook his head, watching Sheriff Ferris stride angrily toward them from his offices up the street. "Who knows?" Frank said. "For now, let's just concentrate on getting through Ferris's interrogation. Then we can go home and sleep on it. Unbelievably, the logs just dented the jeep a little bit."

"I doubt if the rental company will see it that way," Joe pointed out. "It's a good thing we signed up for extra insurance."

Callie Shaw's cry of "Come and get it!" was the first thing Frank heard the next morning when he awoke. He sat up in bed and glanced out the window at the light rainfall, all the time inhaling the wonderful odor of raspberry pancakes.

At first Frank thought Stan must be cooking breakfast again. Then he remembered that Stan had spent the night in jail. He sat up in bed, rubbed his eyes, and looked at Joe asleep in the other twin bed. "Rise and shine," he grumbled good-naturedly. "Today's the day we figure out our case."

"Right." Joe sat up abruptly. "I dreamed we'd solved it already. Easy come, easy go."

When Frank and Joe entered the big, well-equipped kitchen in Stan's cozy cottage, they found Callie and Edgar Morrison, the representative from Save the Redwoods headquarters, just sitting down to breakfast.

"About time you guys wandered in," Callie scolded. "Edgar's been up since six o'clock."

"We had a hard day at the office yesterday," Joe kidded Callie. "Thanks for letting us get our beauty sleep."

"Hurry up and eat." Callie loaded pancakes onto their plates. "Stan will be here in about fifteen minutes."

"What? He's out of jail?" Joe asked through a mouthful of pancake.

"I got him out," Edgar said. "It wasn't all that easy. But working last night and this morning, I finally wore down the sheriff by pointing out that he didn't really have enough evidence to hold Stan. Finally the sheriff agreed to let him go if I stayed out of his face. All Stan had to do was promise to stay in town until the investigation's over."

"Wow." Joe took a more careful look at the young, well-dressed man. He looked the same as he had when Joe and Frank arrived the night before—small, bespectacled, and extremely serious. "When did all this happen?"

"This morning," Callie said briskly, "while you two were dreaming."

"So what's the plan for today?" Frank asked Edgar, reaching for the pitcher of orange juice.

"I assume you three will continue your investigation," Edgar said, "although that has nothing to do with me. My job was to get Stan out of jail and make sure our name hadn't been compromised. I'm done and returning to headquarters this morning. I'll come back, of course, if more trouble develops.''

"Are you a lawyer or something?" Joe asked, squinting sleepily at the trim young man.

"A concerned citizen, that's all," Edgar said, "doing my best for the trees."

Frank grinned. He liked Edgar, even though he appeared a bit stuffy.

Just then they heard a noise at the front door.

"It's him!" Callie said, hurrying to greet her uncle.

A moment later Stan appeared in the kitchen doorway, his head just missing the top of the door frame. "Howdy, folks!" he said cheerily. "I see you've been celebrating my freedom. Think I'll join you."

He sat at the kitchen table and helped himself to pancakes and juice as the others bombarded him with questions. Then they brought him up to date on the investigation.

"Let me show you the photographs of the bootprints," Frank said at last, picking up the second set of prints from the kitchen counter. "They clearly show hobnailed boots, which you weren't wearing. If the sheriff buys our theory that whoever owns these boots killed Owens, then you'll have to be in the clear."

"The only problem," Callie added, "is that the sheriff isn't likely to pay much attention to the theories of Uncle Stan's friends."

While Joe and Callie removed the breakfast plates, Frank spread the photographs out over the kitchen table and began explaining them to Stan and Edgar. Then Joe gave a description of the "accident" with the logging truck.

"You three have done a magnificent job so far," Stan said when they were finished. "I'm really stunned." He rearranged the photographs into a neat pile. "And that's lucky for me because it looks like there's a lot more investigating to do."

"We're willing to help out at headquarters any way we can," Edgar put in.

"Great," Joe said. "Can you do us some background checks and get some police records?"

When Edgar nodded, Frank jumped in. "We need information on Mike Stavisky, a logger for Horizon Lumber; Rafe Collins, Johnson's foreman; and Vance Galen, one of your volunteers."

"Why Vance Galen?" Edgar asked slowly. "Has he been causing more trouble?"

"Not so far as we know," Frank said quickly. He didn't want to rat on Galen about his run-in with the loggers. "But a lot of the loggers think he had something to do with the explosion. Frankly, he's the only person we know who didn't like Owens."

"We don't usually check our volunteers' backgrounds before we send them out in the field," Edgar admitted quietly. "We can't really afford to lose any of them. But I'll check on Galen and the others as soon as I get back to headquarters. Count on it."

"What about me?" Stan asked. "What should I do?"

"You stay here and hold the fort," Frank said politely. "We need someone to take down the information Edgar comes up with. And I'd guess you must be tired and could use a little rest."

"You bet I am. To tell you the truth, I wouldn't mind an hour or so of shut-eye."

"Hey, no problem," Callie said, putting a hand on her uncle's shoulder. "And after your nap you can wash the breakfast dishes."

Five minutes later Frank, Joe, and Callie had said goodbye to Edgar Morrison and Callie's uncle and piled into the Hardys' jeep.

"Where to?" Callie asked from the backseat as Frank drove.

"How about to Walter Ecks's?" Frank asked Callie. "You know—Buster Owens's foreman."

"Walter?" Callie asked. "Okay. But why him?"

Frank met Callie's eyes in the rearview mirror. "I think your uncle's hiding something," he said carefully. "He was too nervous after the questioning last night. And he won't even tell us why he was meeting with Buster."

"I'm sure it was nothing important—" Callie began.

Joe interrupted, "Frank's right. And Walter Ecks was one of the people who Stan said knew about his negotiations with Owens. Ecks is as good a guy to start with as any."

Frank could see that Callie was probably curious about what her uncle was cooking up with Owens about Horizon Lumber. He hoped it wasn't something she'd regret learning.

"Walter lives on Stoner Mountain, just above town." After they drove down Stan's mountain awhile, Callie said, "Turn left. There's a short-cut right around this bend. We don't have to go all the way down into town."

Frank gunned the engine, shifted into the lowest gear, and turned left up the mountain. He grinned at Callie in the rearview mirror as they rounded a sharp bend in the winding road.

"Frank!" Joe yelled.

"What?"

"Look out! Look up ahead!"

Frank stared straight out the windshield. Up ahead, a yellow bulldozer was bearing down on the jeep. And it was moving at top speed!

Chapter
7

"TURN!" Joe shouted. He stared helplessly at the bulldozer, its gleaming blade raised and pointed right at the jeep's windshield.

"What do you think I'm doing?" Frank frantically spun the wheel, just managing to squeeze past the 'dozer. But, to Joe's horror, the jeep slid off the edge of the narrow dirt road.

Callie screamed as the jeep plunged down the mountainside. Like the ball in a pinball game the car bounced from tree to tree, blazing a path through the undergrowth straight to the bottom.

Just when Joe was sure they'd crash and burn, the jeep slammed to a halt, wedged between a boulder and a tree.

For a moment the Hardys and Callie sat surrounded by the silence and caught their breath. Joe finally broke the spell.

"What was *that?*" he demanded, turning in his seat as though he thought the bulldozer might be pursuing them.

But the road wasn't visible above them and no sound broke the silence. Joe could have almost imagined the entire smash-up.

"Is everyone okay?" Joe asked Frank and Callie. They nodded that they were unhurt.

"Then let's unbuckle our seatbelts and get out quick before this thing starts rolling again," Frank said. "You first, Callie."

Callie stumbled out, followed by Joe and Frank, and all three scrambled back up the cliff.

"Well? Was that deliberate?" Callie ventured as the road came into view. The bulldozer was still there, pulled half off the road. As they drew nearer, Joe could see that the driver was gone.

"Maybe," Frank said. "The blade was lifted like he wanted to just sweep us over the edge. And it did a good job of hiding his face so we couldn't identify him."

"But how could he know we were coming?" Joe leaned against the bulldozer to catch his breath.

"Maybe someone's following us," Frank suggested. "Remember last night—those logs that happened to fall right when we were getting in our car?"

"Did you guys notice," Callie asked, pointing at the door, "that it has a Horizon Lumber logo?"

Joe and Frank had already seen the orange-and-purple mark. "That's the second time in two days someone's used Horizon's equipment against us," Joe said. "Seems like someone from Horizon sure wants to scare us away."

Then he noticed that Frank was staring at the ground. "What's up?" he asked his older brother.

"Bootprints." Frank pointed at the dirt by the side of the road near the driver's seat. "My camera's still in the jeep. I'm going to climb down and get it. Sheriff Ferris will need to see some shots of this."

"Are they the same prints you found by Buster's truck?" Callie asked as Frank went off to get the camera.

"There's no way to know," Joe answered. "Both prints were made by hobnailed boots. They look about the same size, but who knows? We'd have to take shots of these and then blow them up to see if they're the same."

"Then let's go ahead and walk up to Walter Ecks's house," Callie suggested. "We can call a tow truck from there. The sooner we get to town, the sooner you guys can develop Frank's film."

After Frank had shot pictures of the bootprints, the Hardys and Callie started up the narrow road toward the cutoff to Stoner Mountain. "It's nice to be hiking, anyway," Callie remarked as they gazed out at the endless vistas of forest that appeared whenever the road took a sharp bend. "After what happened to Uncle Stan I'd given up on hiking."

A short time later Joe glimpsed a neat, cedar-shingled cabin through a break in the bushy green fir trees lining the road. "Is that it?" he asked Callie.

Callie nodded. "Sure is," she said. "And there's Walter himself, sitting on the front porch. I guess he doesn't have much to do now that Horizon's closed down."

Joe spotted the grizzled old man in faded overalls and a dirty white T-shirt, reading the newspaper in the morning sun.

As they approached, an old bloodhound jumped down from the porch and barked until Ecks silenced it with a sharp command.

"Hi there, Callie." Ecks waved to her and seemed to be surprised to see her. "I heard you were back with us this summer. What are you doing all the way up here?"

"Hi, Walt," Callie replied, smiling. "These are my friends Frank and Joe Hardy. We were on our way up to visit you, and our jeep was run off the road by one of Buster's bulldozers."

"What?" Ecks exploded, his face red with anger. "It's those Greens again," he said in a trembling voice. "Horizon has an equipment yard here on Stoner Mountain. Those fanatics aren't satisfied with killing a perfectly good, hardworking lumberjack, I guess. Now they've got to steal our bulldozers and run strangers off mountains!"

"Why would the Greens pull something like that?" Joe asked seriously. "We're not even loggers."

The old man ran a hand across his mouth. His fierce brown eyes glared out at them above a week's worth of whiskers. Joe realized that Ecks had probably been a very tough foreman in his younger days. "They want to scare people," he said. "Callie's uncle is different. But the others who've passed through here . . ." He scowled. "Take that Vance Galen fellow. He's the type to plant bombs in the woods and put spikes in the trees to ruin saw blades. Don't think I haven't seen it happen before!"

"Do you think Galen killed Buster Owens?" Frank asked evenly.

Ecks's mouth dropped open. "Murder's not a word to throw around lightly, son," he said at last. "Galen's reckless—definitely—but I don't know that he's a cold-blooded killer." He turned from Frank to Callie. "What exactly did you want to see me about?" he asked sharply.

"Uncle Stan told us he'd been talking with Owens about a plan for conserving trees," Callie said quickly. "He had a meeting with Buster right before the fire. He didn't mention what it was about, but he said you and Millie Owens knew. We were hoping you could tell us more about it."

Ecks eyed Callie suspiciously. "Why don't you ask your uncle?" he said.

"We did," Joe broke in. "He won't tell us. The problem is, Stan doesn't seem to realize that he needs to clear himself or the sheriff's going to bring charges. I guess your telling us about the meeting would be kind of like saving Stan from himself.''

Ecks shook his head skeptically. "I don't know," he said. "Buster Owens made me swear not to tell anyone. He said there'd be bloodshed if anyone found out. And by golly, maybe there was.''

"Can't you tell us anything?" Callie asked.

Ecks hesitated. Then he sighed. "I'll tell you this much. It has something to do with that Forest Service contract that's coming up soon. Stan was helping Buster work out a way to win it.''

Callie frowned. "That doesn't sound so dangerous—except maybe to someone who wants that contract, too.''

Ecks shrugged. "If you ask me, girl, you three are looking in the wrong place for answers. This death's got nothing to do with that plan. If I were you, I'd go back over to the scene of the crime and check for clues. Isn't that the way it works in detective novels?" he added. "The criminal returns to the scene of the crime?''

Joe started to answer, but just then Walter's bloodhound jumped to its feet, pointed its nose toward the road, and started barking.

"Now, what set that fool dog off?" Ecks wondered as the bloodhound raced for the edge of the yard. "Must be a rabbit.''

The Hardys, Callie, and Walter Ecks peered in the direction the bloodhound was running. "Hope it's not a skunk," Ecks added.

Suddenly Joe saw a flash of movement in the

branches of a tall fir tree on the edge of the woods. "Hey—there's somebody out there!" he shouted, setting off toward the forest. "Maybe it's someone spying!"

"There he goes!" Frank called from behind him. Joe glimpsed a figure in camouflage clothes leaping down from the trees and running off into the forest. "Come on!" he called to the others.

"Be careful!" Callie shouted as she and Frank took off after Joe. "He might have a gun!"

Joe ran as fast as he could after the fleeing figure. He leapt over fallen trees and small boulders, hoping the low ferns and tree stumps wouldn't trip him up as he closed in on the man.

Finally, Joe could hear the heavy tread and ragged breathing of the camouflaged man about twenty yards ahead. Forcing himself through the undergrowth, he tried to run faster. Behind him, Frank and Callie crashed along the path he had beaten down.

Then, suddenly, Joe could no longer hear the footsteps and panting of his quarry. Before he could think about where the man might have gone, he heard something heavy drop to the ground behind him.

"Where'd you—" he cried out, spinning to face his enemy.

But he failed to make it all the way around. Something heavy and hard smashed down on the back of his head, and Joe tumbled headfirst onto a carpet of leaves.

Chapter

8

"JOE! Are you all right?" Frank plunged toward his brother. Joe lay half hidden behind an enormous tree trunk.

"Oh," Joe groaned, struggling to sit up as Frank knelt at his side. "What happened? My head is killing me."

"It looks like our spy has a violent streak," Frank said, inspecting the back of Joe's head. "Fortunately, he didn't have time to do much damage. It looks like just a bump. The swelling will probably go down in a couple of hours."

"That's easy for you to say." Joe rubbed his head gingerly. "It's going to seem like a couple of months to me."

"I say we go back to Walter Ecks's place," Callie said as she joined them. "Whoever that creep was, he's long gone by now. And we need to get some ice on that bump."

"Fine by me." Frank helped his brother up. "Did you get a look at the guy before he brained you, Joe?"

"Not his face," Joe answered. "Just a bit of his sleeve, which was a camouflage shirt. And I had the impression he was about average height. Not quite as tall as me."

"Do you think it could have been Vance Galen?" Callie asked as they made their way back down the path to Ecks's cabin. "We saw him wearing camouflage."

"Plenty of guys must wear camouflage around here," Frank said. "So we can't be *sure* who it was. Besides, we saw the guy yesterday at the newspaper office. He didn't act like we were the enemy then."

"Yeah, but that was before he saw us talking to Buster's foreman," Callie pointed out. "Maybe he thinks we've hooked up with the bad guys."

"Maybe whoever bonked Joe doesn't think anything—maybe he was just trying to get away," Frank reasoned.

When they rejoined Walter Ecks and the older man had brought out ice to reduce the swelling on Joe's head, Walter agreed with Callie.

"There are only half a dozen cabins in this area," he said. "Galen's is the closest. Of course, that doesn't mean it had to be him, but like I say, he's as crazy as they come."

Frank accepted a glass of lemonade from Walter and passed one to Callie.

"The guy who attacked me was going off to

the right,'' Joe said, thinking out loud. He gestured with his hand. ''Uphill, I guess, right over that way.''

''That's the way to Galen's cabin!'' Ecks said excitedly. ''Just about a mile past Horizon's equipment yard.''

Suddenly Joe grinned.

''Something funny?'' Frank asked.

''Not really, but that bump on the head must have shaken something loose. I just realized what it was that was missing from Buster Owens's belongings.''

''What?'' Callie asked, taking a sip of lemonade.

''His key ring!'' Joe exclaimed. ''He had the biggest key ring I've ever seen hanging from his belt at the general store. You could hardly help but notice the thing. Maybe whoever killed Buster took his keys.''

''What did the keys open, Walt?'' Callie asked, her expression very serious.

''Oh, just about everything,'' Ecks replied. ''All the equipment yards, for one thing. And the buildings down at the mill. He had the keys to all the vehicles, too. He used to say he didn't trust the loggers not to lose them.''

For an instant Walter Ecks's eyes teared up. Embarrassed, he wiped the tears away. ''Nobody but Buster had every key,'' he added. ''I have a few for the mill and yard, and Millie has some for their house, of course. But Buster had every single key on that ring. He liked to keep stuff to himself.''

"Thanks, Walt," Callie said a bit later, after they took the empty lemonade glasses inside to the kitchen. "I think we should go talk to Vance Galen."

"On the way let's check out the equipment yard to see if anything's missing," Joe put in. "Do you have an inventory list so we can check to see if anything's gone?"

Ecks gave Joe a list and a key to the gate. He offered to call the towing company for their car and have it brought into Crosscut. The Hardys and Callie said goodbye and set off up the mountain road, this time keeping a sharp eye out for attackers.

"Getting run off the road by a bulldozer and pounced on by a stranger in the woods sure does help a guy work up an appetite," Joe muttered as they trudged on under the hot sun. It was past noon, and the heat was becoming uncomfortable even that high in the mountains.

"Don't worry," Frank said. "We'll put some fuel in that body the minute we finish with Galen."

"If he turns out to be the guy who attacked me," Joe added, "maybe I'll just have him for lunch."

The lock on the equipment yard gate showed no signs of tampering. "That means if something was taken from here, it was done by someone with a key," Frank pointed out, unlocking the gate. "Okay, fan out. The inventory says there should be eight bulldozers here. If there's one missing, it shouldn't be hard to spot.''

"There's one bulldozer missing," Callie called out a few minutes later. "But nothing else is gone, as far as we can see," she added as she and Joe rejoined Frank near the gate. "What are you looking for?" she asked when she saw Frank peering at the ground.

"Bootprints," he said, frowning. "But the mud's too stirred up to tell anything."

"What more evidence do we need?" Joe demanded. "Vance Galen lives near here. He could easily have come in here and snitched a 'dozer, that logging truck that unloaded on us last night, and even a few sticks of dynamite. I think we have a suspect, Frank."

"Patience, brother," Frank said. "Let's go talk to the guy first before we decide he's guilty."

"Not home," Joe announced when no one answered Frank's knock on Galen's door. "Must be out bulldozing cars again."

"Come on," said Callie dejectedly. "Let's go home."

"Hold on," Frank insisted, knocking again. "Galen!" he called. The silence that answered his call was eerie.

Frank reached out and tried the doorknob. "You're just going to walk in?" Callie demanded.

"Nope. It's locked," Frank said, disappointed.

"I guess it would be hard to break in and say we just wandered by."

"On the other hand, Stan's life *is* at stake here," Joe pointed out, eyeing his brother over Callie's head. "And it's not like we're going to take anything."

Callie studied first one Hardy then the other. She knew better than to argue when she saw that determined look in their eyes. "Okay, but hurry." She glanced at the edges of the woods in case Galen appeared and caught them in the act. "And remember, this is quick and unofficial. Whatever we see stays right where it was."

It took only moments for Frank to work the door lock with the slender pick he kept in his wallet. He heard the final tumbler click into place. Then, motioning for Callie and Joe to follow, he went inside.

"What a dump," Joe said the instant they were inside the small, dimly lit cabin. It definitely could use a cleaning, Frank saw. Dirty clothes, books, and newspapers covered every flat surface. The tiny kitchen had dishes stacked to the rim of the sink. The windows were tightly shut, preventing any fresh mountain air coming into the rooms.

"Look for anything that might connect Galen to the bombing at the sawmill," Frank told the others, moving through the living room toward a tiny bedroom and bathroom off a short hall.

"Especially Buster's key ring," Joe added,

opening several cabinets in the living room. "That would clinch it for sure."

Frank entered Galen's bedroom and saw several sets of camouflage pants and shirts tossed around. If anyone in Crosscut could be associated with camouflage, Galen was certainly the one.

At the bottom of Galen's closet, though, Frank found something even more interesting: a small door that concealed a hidden compartment beneath the floor. Inside were two boxes of blasting caps, several coils of waterproof fuse, some well-thumbed military handbooks, and a demolition instruction manual.

"Joe! Callie!" Frank called. "Come here!"

"You come here!" Joe called back from the living room. "This guy has enough weapons to supply the National Guard!"

Frank hurried out of the bedroom to find Joe standing over a hole in the floor near the living room fireplace. Several floorboards lay nearby. "Let's see, there's one pump shotgun and a high-powered rifle," Joe said, peering down into the hole.

"And some boxes of ammo and several pistols," Frank added, kneeling beside Joe. "It looks like our friend Galen is getting ready to start a war."

"All he needs is the dynamite," Callie said.

"Wait till you see what's in the bedroom." Frank described to the other two what he had found.

"Whew," Joe said. "This guy really sounds crazy."

"I guess he might be capable of committing murder—and framing Uncle Stan," Callie agreed sadly.

"Let's put everything back the way we found it," Frank said hastily. "We don't want Galen to know he's been found out. I want to report this to the sheriff so he can bring this guy in for questioning."

"You really think he'd notice something missing in this mess?" Joe asked.

"Hey, look at your room at home!" Frank replied, only half kidding. "And still you know every time I borrow a pair of socks from your dresser."

Frank, Joe, and Callie worked quickly to restore Galen's cabin to its original state. As they worked, Frank fought down a feeling of nervousness about what they'd been up to. One thing was sure—going through Galen's personal belongings was not something he wanted to be caught doing.

"Okay, out!" he ordered Callie and Joe, hustling them toward the door as soon as the last dirty shirt was back in place. Frank backed out after them, careful to lock the door.

"Wait!" Joe said just as Frank felt the lock click. "I think I left the car keys on the mantel."

"You're kidding." Frank was incredulous, but Joe only shrugged sheepishly. "They're not in my pocket," he said.

Shaking his head, Frank moved to the window and shined his flashlight through the glass. "I don't see them," he said. "Maybe you left them in the—"

He was interrupted by the click of a rifle bolt and Callie's gasp of fright.

"Don't move," said a high-pitched voice behind and to the right of Frank. Slowly Frank raised his hands and turned to face Vance Galen.

The Green, in suspenders and a red flannel shirt, stared triumphantly into Frank's eyes. His hunting rifle was leveled at Callie's heart, and his finger was trembling on the trigger.

Chapter

9

"TAKE IT EASY, Vance," Joe murmured. "We're not trying to hurt you."

"This is private property," Galen snarled. "You're trespassing!"

"Vance, if you'll just listen, I can explain," Callie said calmly, taking a step toward him.

"Careful, Callie," Frank warned.

"Shut up, Hardy!" Galen shouted, his finger tightening around the trigger.

"It's okay," Callie said soothingly. "We just want to talk." She walked closer to him. "Put down the rifle."

Callie kept walking until she was right up against the barrel of his rifle. The boys held their breath. Finally Galen lowered it.

"Let's talk inside," he muttered.

As they stepped back to let Galen unlock the

door, Joe noted that Galen seemed more scared than anything. He just hoped Galen stayed that way.

"All right," Galen said after they had filed into the living room and sat down. "I want to know why you were spying on me."

"We weren't spying," Frank protested. "We needed to talk to you, but you didn't appear to be here. We were just looking inside for you."

"Don't lie to me!" Still clutching his rifle, Galen glared at Frank. "You boys have something to do with Buster Owens's murder, and I want to know what it is."

"Us!" Joe laughed. "All we're trying to do is prove that Stan Shaw didn't commit it! Do you think you could help us out with that, Vance?"

"What can I do?" Galen growled, beginning to pace. "Everyone around here thinks I'm either loony or a murderer."

"We just need some simple information," Callie said. "Like, what happened with Stan and Buster after we left the general store?"

Galen scowled. "Buster left right after you did," he told her.

"Did Stan say anything about a meeting with Buster?" Joe asked.

"Yeah," Galen replied. "I followed Stan to his car. He said he was going to go over the application for the Forest Service contract with Buster. I told him he was making a big mistake."

"It was a mistake to talk to a logger about conserving woodland?" Frank asked, incredulous.

"You can't trust any mill owner!" Galen spat out. "All they care about is how much money they can make by destroying forests!"

"What happened after you talked to Stan?" Callie asked.

"He wouldn't call off the meeting," Galen said, "so I decided to follow him."

"Then you were there right before the explosion?" Joe asked. "Did you see Stan there?"

"No. I parked away from the mill, on a back road, and walked. I was afraid there might be a guard at the mill."

"Did you park near Buster's truck?" Joe asked.

"No. I saw it, though."

"And then what, Vance?" Callie prodded. "Did you see anyone else around there?"

Joe watched carefully as Galen backed away from them. "I might've seen something," he admitted. "But why should I tell you?"

"Because we're trying to find out who really blew up the sawmill and killed Buster!" Callie cried. Joe flinched. Callie had to cool it. "If you know something important, you should tell us or the sheriff," she added.

"Tell *Ferris?*" Galen exploded. "He'd never believe me! He probably thinks *I* helped blow up the mill!"

"Has he questioned you?" Frank asked.

"Nope," Galen replied, "and he's not going to. I'm not giving him any excuse to lock me up."

"What did you see near the sawmill?" Joe asked again. "A person? Somebody's car?"

Joe saw Galen jerk slightly at the word *car*. Frank saw it, too.

"Whose car was it, Vance? Who else are you afraid of?" Frank asked.

Galen sat down uneasily on the edge of a chair and faced the Hardys. He laid the rifle across his knees.

"All right," he said finally. "I thought I saw Rafe Collins's Cadillac parked off the road. It's a red sixty-seven, a beat-up old wreck that Collins is real proud of. It's hard to miss. Buster's truck was parked right by it," he said finally.

"Collins? Bo Johnson's foreman? You actually saw him there?" Joe jumped in.

Galen shook his head. "I didn't see anybody. Just the truck and the car. Then, right afterward came the explosion. I was so close, I was stunned by it. I wandered away and eventually found my truck."

"What happened after that?" Frank asked.

"I went home. Ever since that day, I've been scared."

"Of Collins?" Callie asked him.

"Absolutely. Once, after I organized some roadblocks on Johnson Lumber's logging roads, he told me he'd shoot me if I ever set foot on Johnson property again. I believe he'd do it, too. Bo Johnson hired him straight out of prison on a work-release parole to keep the mill employees in line."

"What do you mean?" Frank asked.

"You know," Galen said, "if Johnson's employees get any notions about saving the local wildlife or joining a union, Collins leans on them."

Neither of the Hardys believed all of what Galen said, but their impression of Collins coincided pretty well with his description.

"Did you have any more plans for sabotaging the lumber companies?" Frank asked. "Anything that might involve dynamite, for example?"

Galen sat up straight, gripping his rifle more tightly. "Did you come in here earlier?"

"Relax, Vance," Joe said calmly. "We're just trying to help Stan—and *you*, if you'll let us."

Galen slowly relaxed his grip on the rifle. "All right," he said. "I did get a bunch of books on dynamite and some fuses and other stuff back when the state legislature decided to let the redwoods be cut. I was going to get some dynamite and blow up the access roads."

"But the legislature voted to save the trees," Callie pointed out.

"It's a good thing," Galen said quietly. "I don't know if I would have had the guts to blow anything up. Collins has me too scared to fight Johnson Lumber, and they're the worst mill in the state. So all I do is talk."

"As long as it's good talk, it's worthwhile," Frank suggested. "Will you tell Ferris about seeing Collins's car when we're ready to bring our evidence to him?"

Galen hesitated. The Hardys could see the inner battle he was fighting. After a short pause Galen's conscience apparently won out over his fear. "Okay. I'll talk to Ferris."

"Great. Now, there's just one more thing we need from you, Vance," Joe said.

"What's that?" he asked wearily.

"A ride down the mountain."

It was late afternoon by the time the Hardys and Callie reached the general store. Vance waved goodbye and said he was going to visit Stan. Joe spotted their jeep parked in front—a little beat up, but not too bad, considering. "I wonder if it works." He hurried over and checked. Sure enough, it started right up. A sign taped to the steering wheel read, "Ten bucks for towing off the mountain. Leave the money at the general store."

"Now that's the kind of small-town hospitality I like," Joe said. "Let's go inside and pay the guy. And after a quick bite, how about checking out the site of the explosion? There's probably no one around today, and something might turn up."

"Sounds good to me," Frank said, moving toward the general store.

"Wow. It looks so sad," Callie said as they drove into the parking lot. Only two warehouses were untouched by the fire.

"Let's start near that big saw, the one the

85

arson investigators were talking about,'' Frank said as they hopped out of the jeep. "That is, if we can figure out where it was in this mess.''

Silently they crossed the parking lot to the rubble that had been the main building. Joe instantly found what had to be the mill's largest saw. The jagged-toothed steel plate, at least ten feet in diameter, had been bent nearly in half.

"No fire would have done that," Frank said, resting a hand on the ruined saw. "That would take a lot of explosives—probably dynamite.''

"There are plenty of footprints here," Joe said, pointing to the ash-covered ground around the saw. "Fire fighters, paramedics, the arson investigators—too many to identify.''

"I'm glad I wasn't inside fighting the fire,'' Callie commented as they poked around. "It must have been horribly hot. Hey,'' she added, squatting down to peer beneath the saw's cradle. "I think I found something.''

Callie retrieved something from under the cradle and stood up. When she opened her hand there was a battered steel cigarette lighter.

"Hmm. Not very impressive,'' Callie said. "One of the mill workers must have dropped it.''

Joe took the lighter and turned it over. A bit of brass was tacked to the other side. "Wings over a parachute. Isn't that some kind of military insignia?''

"Right, for the army paratroopers,'' said Frank. He took the lighter and scraped the ashes off the bottom. "Uh-huh,'' he added. "There's an inscription here. It says, 'Saigon, seventy-two.' Whoever dropped this is probably a Vietnam veteran. It shouldn't be too hard to find out if there are any ex-paratroopers who work at the mill. If the owner of the lighter can't explain how his lighter got here, we just might have our man."

"I don't know, Frank," Callie said with a frown. "It's pretty flimsy."

"It's all we have to go on so far," said Frank, irritation creeping into his voice. "Let's look around and see if anything else turns up."

Joe turned back to sifting through the ashes until he heard Frank say, "Okay, I give up. If we haven't found anything by now, there's nothing else to find."

"Including Buster's keys," Joe pointed out.

"Right." Frank nodded. "Which means either the investigators found them—"

"Or the murderer took them," Joe finished grimly. "Which explains why Horizon's equipment keeps following us around."

"Let's go back to town. I could eat again," Callie suggested, dusting ash off her hands. "Maybe Peg Robbins at the general store can tell us who owns that lighter. She knows everyone in town, and Uncle Stan says she loves to gab."

By the time the Hardys and Callie returned to the general store, it was nearly dusk and the lunch counter was empty. Only breakfast and lunch were served. Portly Peg Robbins, whom they had watched serving the loggers the day before, stood behind the counter wiping down the coffee machine. Her husband sat in his usual spot behind the cash register, this time working a crossword puzzle. The teenagers headed straight for the single rest room in the back, taking turns cleaning up as best they could.

"Hi, Peg," Callie said as they finally climbed onto the stools in front of the counter. "Do you remember me? Callie Shaw, Stan's niece?"

"Of course I do!" the woman cried, turning around and giving Callie a big, motherly smile. "I never forget a soul who passes through this old place." Her face turned somber as she stepped closer, wiping her hands on a dishcloth. "My dear, I'm so sorry about your poor uncle," she said gravely. "Can I get you anything—we're officially closed but I make lots of exceptions."

Callie waited until Peg served them to strike up a conversation again. Finally, she held up the paratrooper lighter.

"We found this yesterday when we were hiking," Callie said casually. "It looks like it might be important to someone, so we thought we'd bring it here to see if you might recognize it. We'd like to get it back to its owner if we can."

"Of course," she said. "Mike Stavisky's your man. He went to Vietnam with the paratroopers in—let's see—May of 1971. He was discharged in 1972. I remember his mother's excitement when he got off that bus like it was yesterday."

"Mike Stavisky?" Joe tried to hide his excitement. "Are you sure, ma'am?"

"Of course I'm sure!" Peg Robbins drew herself up to her full height. "Michael's used that lighter at this counter a hundred times. It's a real keepsake, this is." She smiled at Callie. "He'll appreciate getting it back."

"Uh, do you know where we might find him?" Frank asked.

A wry smile appeared on Peg Robbins's lips. "I have a very good idea," she said smugly. "Though I'm not sure I should tell."

"Of course you should," Callie said, coaxing her.

Peg hesitated only one more second before she leaned her elbows on the counter and whispered to them. "Well, don't tell them I told you," she said. "But with poor Buster Owens out of the picture, I'd bet the store that Mike's over at Millie Owens's right now."

"Millie Owens?" Joe said, surprised.

Meg nodded importantly. "I happen to know that Mike's been smitten with that girl since high school. For years he's been after her to marry him. But her dad wouldn't hear of it, and he was Mike's boss. Now, though, Buster's no longer in the way."

Peg straightened up, smoothed her apron over her dress, and glanced guiltily toward her husband. "Now," she said in a much louder voice, "how about some of my famous blackberry pie?"

"Turn left here," Callie said from the passenger seat of the jeep as Joe steered down a dark mountain road. She held Frank's pocket penlight close to the paper on which she'd scrawled Peg Robbins's directions to Millie's house.

"Just a couple of miles more," she said. "Then a right at the Owenses' mailbox, and Millie's house is about half a mile farther on."

"Boy, the Owenses really like their privacy," Frank remarked from the backseat as the jeep made its way through the deepening gloom. A few minutes later he added, "Look. I see lights through the trees."

"We're in luck," Callie observed. "Millie must be home."

The dirt road suddenly dipped as it went around a sharp corner, and Joe lost sight of the house. But as he drove out of the dip, he heard the sounds of angry shouting.

"Do you hear that?" he asked Callie. "It sounds like two people fighting."

Callie rolled down her window to hear better. The shouts came again. Then Joe heard a scream.

"Did you hear what I heard?" Joe asked Callie.

She was staring at the house, her eyes wide. "Step on it, Joe!" she yelled. "Millie's in trouble!"

Chapter

10

INSTINCTIVELY Joe's foot slammed down on the accelerator. The jeep flew the final fifty yards to the Owenses' home. Frank caught a quick glimpse of thinning trees and a sprawling ranch house. Joe braked the jeep to a grinding halt beside a rusty pickup parked at the end of the drive.

Frank jumped out onto the lawn.

"The scream came from the house," Callie said, running toward the house with Joe following. "See? The front door's open."

Light glowed through the curtains covering a picture window at the front of the house. Frank could see two figures silhouetted against the curtains. One was tall and clearly female; the other was somewhat shorter, stockier, and male.

"Stay away from me!" Frank heard a female

voice cry as he raced to the front door. "I told you, Mike, it's over between us!"

"But, Millie, I did it for you!"

Frank recognized Mike Stavisky's voice. As he reached the door, he saw Mike's silhouette advance toward the woman's. She backed away and screamed again.

"All right, that's enough!" Frank shouted, bursting through the open doorway, Joe and Callie right behind him.

Mike Stavisky stared at the teenagers in open-mouthed amazement. The tall, plain-faced woman who'd been arguing with him was speechless, too. Her resemblance to Buster Owens left no doubt that she was his daughter, Millie.

"Clear off!" Stavisky finally growled, his face above the beard and mustache a bright red. "This is none of your business!"

"We're making it our business, friend," Joe said, moving closer. "We could hear Ms. Owens scream all the way out in the driveway."

"I'm okay." Millie clutched a handkerchief as though she wanted to tear it to pieces. Frank noticed that the room in which they were standing was filled with expensive-looking antiques. A large fireplace was set into one wall, and the other walls were hung with paintings. Clearly, the mill had earned a big income for the Owens family.

"Mike and I were just having a—a difference of opinion. And Mike's leaving. Aren't you, Mike?"

"No, I'm not leaving," Stavisky said, still red-faced. "Why should I? Because a bunch of Stan Shaw's buddies try to throw me out? I have a right to stay here until we settle things, Millie, and you know it!"

"What's there to settle?" Millie said sharply, forgetting the others for a moment. "The mill is mine now. My father's estate will be settled in the next few months. And if you want to keep your job, Mike, you'd better start speaking to me with more respect."

Millie's words left Stavisky sputtering. Before Mike could recover, Joe patted his pockets absentmindedly and said, "Hey, Mike, got a light?"

"Sure . . ." Without turning his gaze from Millie, Stavisky reached into the pocket of his jeans. Then his expression changed. "Hey," he said, momentarily distracted, "where's my—"

"Looking for this?" Frank held up the lighter they'd found at the mill.

"Yeah, it's mine." He made a quick grab for the lighter, but Frank snatched it out of his reach.

"We thought so," Frank said. "We found this underneath the big saw at the Horizon mill— about ten yards from where Mr. Owens's body was found."

Millie's jaw dropped open as she stared at Stavisky. "Mike," she said in a horrified voice. "You didn't—"

93

"So I dropped it there!" Stavisky protested loudly. "I work at the mill! Big deal!"

"You work at the mill," Millie said slowly, "but not anywhere near the saw. You cut trees, right, Mike? You don't saw planks."

"So what? I was in there the other day, talking to your dad! What do you take me for, Millie, a murderer?"

Stavisky stared at Millie. She stared back. As Frank, Callie, and Joe watched, Stavisky started backing slowly toward the door.

"Hold it, Mike," Joe said. "We're not finished talking to you."

"Oh, yeah?" Stavisky made a sudden lunge to his left, grabbing a poker from the fireplace tools on the hearth. He waved it threateningly at the Hardys.

"You think you can barge in here and wreck my life," Mike said, barely coherent. "You Greens always think you know everything. You're always willing to sacrifice everyone's happiness but your own. Well, you've got the wrong guy, buddy. Nobody's going to put Mike Stavisky in jail."

"Mike, put the poker down," Joe coaxed, stepping closer.

"Stay back!" Mike yelled, and he opened the door with one hand and sent the poker flying right toward Joe's head.

"Hey!" Joe ducked as the poker whizzed overhead. Millie screamed as it sailed past her shoulder, and landed harmlessly in the carpet at the far end of the room.

"That's not funny, Mike!" Joe yelled, checking the top of his head to make sure his hair didn't have a new part. Mike flung open the door and raced outside. "You won't get far!" Joe shouted after him.

"I don't have to!" the enraged veteran shouted over his shoulder as he took off for his truck. Opening the door, he jumped inside before anyone could catch up with him. As Millie joined the three on the front lawn, Stavisky backed the truck onto the dirt drive. "You haven't heard the last of me, Millie!" he yelled out the open window. "Not until I get what's owed me!" Then he jammed the truck in gear and disappeared into the darkness.

Frank turned to Millie Owens. "What was that all about?" he asked.

"Maybe I'll tell you," Millie countered sharply, "after you tell me who you are."

"They're friends of mine," Callie said to her. "I'm Callie Shaw, Stan Shaw's niece. This is Frank Hardy, my boyfriend, and that's his brother, Joe. They're helping me try to clear my uncle of the charges that he . . ."

"Killed my dad?" Millie said harshly.

Callie frowned, then looked the woman in the eye. "You know they were friends," she said carefully. "You don't think my uncle Stan would have killed Buster, do you?"

Millie glared at her for a moment, then relented. "No," she admitted. "Much as I'd like to blame someone, I don't believe Stan's the one."

"Good." Joe stepped closer to her. "Then maybe you won't mind telling us what your fight with Mike was about?"

Millie's face quickly resumed its stonelike expression. "That was a personal matter," she said coldly. "Mike and I used to be, well—close. The trouble is, he didn't accept it when things cooled off. I got tired of fighting with my father about Mike. He never approved of him for me, so I finally decided to give Mike up. He wasn't worth the trouble to me anymore." She made a wry face. "I had trouble convincing him, though, as you could see."

"Do you think he could have killed your father?" Joe asked quietly. "We heard they didn't get along."

She shook her head, mystified. "I've known Mike since fourth grade. I never would have suspected he was capable of such a thing. But just a week ago, he wrote me a letter."

"A love letter?" Callie asked.

Millie grimaced. "Sort of. I'd broken up with him for good the day before. In the letter he said he'd do anything to get me back. He knew I'd always wanted to run Horizon Mill myself. Dad never would let me, and Mike used to boast that when we were married, we'd take over the mill and run it together, even steven. But I still can't believe he'd—he'd—" she stammered.

Then she got hold of herself. "Let's go inside," she said. "I don't know what would have happened if you hadn't shown up. The least I can do is offer you all some hot chocolate."

"What I don't understand," Callie said as they followed Millie into the Owenses' spacious kitchen, "is why Mike would act against your father *now*—assuming that he did anything. Your relationship had been going on for a long time, right? And you'd broken up with him, so it was really too late."

"He might have been scared Dad would fire him," Millie theorized as she put milk to heat on the stove. "He'd just fired Mike's best friend, Freddy Zackarias. He caught Freddy stealing stuff at the mill. Mike might have thought he'd be next, and then he'd have no excuse to hang around me."

She opened a cabinet and brought out a box of cocoa. "I don't believe it, though. Mike wouldn't be able to kill anyone in cold blood. There's something deeper behind my father's death. I just wish I could figure out what."

For the first time Frank thought the tall, sturdy woman might break down and cry. "We'll try to help you find out," he said gently. "We're as anxious to clear Callie's uncle as you are to find the real murderer."

Millie smiled weakly and nodded. Then, as she passed around the mugs of chocolate, Joe asked, "Millie, can you tell us what Freddy stole from the mill? It might give us a lead on what to look for."

"Nothing much, that I know of," Millie said, surprised. "He was caught in my dad's office. Dad didn't keep valuables there. The payroll is issued straight from the bank. I heard they caught Freddy with a book of Dad's personal checks in his pocket. To tell you the truth," she said dryly, "Freddy Zackarias isn't very smart."

Joe remembered Stavisky's shrill-voiced, stringy-haired sidekick. Then he asked, "Were any keys stolen?"

When Millie turned to him, he explained. "We found out today that someone's apparently using a set of Horizon's keys to help himself to the company's equipment. Your father's keys are missing—we searched the mill today, and they weren't there. If you can account for all your copies of the keys, then the thief must have your father's key ring. And whoever has that key ring is probably the person who killed your father."

Millie turned pale. "I'll have to make sure mine are still here. I'll be right back."

It didn't take long for Millie to locate her own key collection. "Nothing's missing," she informed the boys. "I'm sure the only copies were with me and Walter Ecks—"

"And we checked with Walter earlier," Callie broke in. "He has his keys, too. That means—"

"The only missing keys are the ones taken from Owens himself," Joe said excitedly. "If we can locate that key ring, chances are we've found our killer!"

The loud ring of the telephone caused them all to jump. Millie walked over to answer it.

"Hello?" she said into the receiver. Then her face darkened. "Oh, yes. My father told me he was due in today. He's late, isn't he?"

As Frank sipped his chocolate and watched her, Millie listened to the caller for a moment. Then her eyes widened.

"What?" she demanded.

She listened for a few more moments, then said abruptly, "Stay where you are. I'm going to get in touch with our foreman, then I'll call you back. And I want to know if you hear anything else!"

Millie hung up the phone and turned to the others.

"Bad news?" Callie asked, concerned.

Millie threw up her hands. "That was one of our loggers, down at the Sportsman. He says the truck driver who's delivering the first load of new equipment for the mill just stopped in for a bite to eat. He says they got a call from Johnson's mill this morning. Johnson told them not to bother delivering the new equipment to our mill. He said we couldn't afford to pay for it now that the buildings have burned down. He told them I'd agreed to sell the stuff to him at a decent price, so they should just deliver the stuff to him!"

Chapter

11

"WHY WOULD SOMEONE do that?" Callie demanded, sitting forward in her chair.

"Because Johnson's greedy," Millie said bitterly. "He set up business here ten years ago, and he hasn't played fair since. Every time my dad found a good worker, Johnson tried to hire him away. If my dad heard of some new forest land up for lease, Johnson would grab it first. But this is the last straw."

Millie sighed. "I'm going to have a talk with Walter Ecks," she said briskly. "It'll probably last awhile. I don't mean to be rude, but—"

"I guess we'd better leave," Frank said quickly. "Thanks for the hot chocolate."

As soon as they were outside, Frank added, "Well, that was interesting. What do you think Millie will do?"

"Wait for the insurance money and rebuild, is my guess," said Joe.

"Do you think Mike Stavisky killed her father?" Callie ventured as they climbed back into the jeep.

"I don't know," Frank answered thoughtfully. "At first I was sure he'd done it. Now I'm not sure."

"He seemed crazy enough to me," Joe remarked from the back seat.

Frank gunned the engine. "Maybe. But that phone call Millie received has me wondering about Johnson's mill. There may be more to this than healthy competition."

"Fine. But for now, we go home," Callie insisted.

"Right." Frank started the engine. "Let's hope Stan got those background checks on Collins, Stavisky, and Zackarias from the home office."

The instant the Hardys and Callie turned the last bend and saw Stan's cabin they knew there was trouble. Cars were parked for a hundred yards in front of the house, and about a dozen people lounged on the lawn. The front door was shut tight, though, and Stan was nowhere to be seen.

"Who are these people?" Callie asked.

"Either your uncle invited all his friends for a party," Joe said, "or a bunch of reporters have decided Stan is the story of the week."

Joe knew the answer to the question the instant he stepped out of the jeep.

"Hi there!" one of the reporters said loudly, approaching Joe with pen and notebook in hand. "Are you friends of Mr. Shaw's? Can you comment on how he feels, being a prime suspect for the crime of murder?"

"Has Save the Redwoods canned him yet?" shouted another reporter, running to join her colleague. Joe realized, as they reached the front porch, that the entire group was now in hot pursuit of them.

A microphone was jabbed into Callie's face. "What made Stan Shaw burn a man to death in his own mill?" a reporter demanded at the top of her lungs.

Before Callie or the Hardys could react, the front door swung open. All three of them ducked inside just before the door was slammed shut.

Dazed, Joe turned to see a disheveled-looking Stan Shaw standing behind them in the vestibule. He had on pajamas and a robe, but he looked as if he hadn't slept in a week.

"That was unbelievable!" Callie cried as they followed Stan into the living room.

"You're telling me," Stan said, sinking down into his desk chair. "When the first one rang the doorbell I got up and answered it." He smiled wearily. "The guy was interviewing me before I had the door completely open. 'Do you believe in murdering for the environment, Mr. Shaw?' "

His eyes met Joe's. "I honestly think he

wanted me to answer yes. Anything that would have sold copies of his paper."

Joe nodded. "Have you heard from the sheriff's office?" he asked Stan.

"Just once. The sheriff called to make sure I was sticking close to home," Stan said wryly. "They're counting on the arson investigators' report to put me back behind bars."

"Stan." Frank leaned forward in the armchair he'd taken near the fireplace. "It would really help our investigation if you could fill us in on that meeting you had with Buster Owens before he died."

Stan Shaw frowned. "I'm sorry, but that information's still confidential," he insisted. "I really don't believe it has anything to do with Buster's death. No one knew what the meeting was about but a few trusted associates. Sorry, but that subject has to be closed."

There was an awkward silence, which Stan finally broke. "I'm sorry I can't cooperate more. But I promise you, that meeting was not important. Now, tell me what you did find out today."

Frank and Callie quickly related their adventures to the attentive environmentalist. When they'd finished, Stan nodded thoughtfully and said, "All this is very interesting, but I see what you mean when you say it's inconclusive. Personally, I have a very bad feeling about Mike Stavisky. But then we Greens have had so many run-ins with him.

"As far as my assistant, Vance Galen, goes . . ."

Stan grimaced. "I guess it's hard to tell who's crazier, him or Mike," he admitted. "Tonight I had to order him to stay in town to keep him from attacking those reporters out front. You can make up your own minds about these characters. Edgar faxed me background checks on both of them, plus one on Rafe Collins."

He tossed Joe a stack of papers and returned to his desk chair. Joe scanned the first page. "Galen's rap sheet shows a few arrests. But they're all for disorderly conduct at protest marches. Nothing serious."

"Try the next one," Frank said.

Joe picked up the next page in the stack. "Mike Stavisky's file," he said. After a moment's reading he added, "It's pretty much like Galen's, really, except that Stavisky's a vet. He was hit with a few public-nuisance-type charges right after his discharge from the military. Then just years of work in the lumber business right around here."

Joe flipped to the next page. "Rafe Collins," he read. He scanned the small type for a moment. "Robbery. Assault. Assault. This is *not* a nice man."

"What's his job record?" Frank asked.

Joe scanned the data. "Grocery clerk, mechanic. Nothing to do with logging."

"Then why did Johnson hire him?" Callie wondered.

"I can tell you that," Stan said. "The rumor is that Johnson hired Collins to keep the employees in line. That's Johnson's idea of employer-employee relations."

"I heard that rumor, too," Frank told him. "But I don't know what it has to do with Buster Owens."

"For starters, why would Johnson hire a goon like him if he wasn't up to something shady?"

"Wait a minute." Frank's eyes lit up. "Is there anything more you can tell us about the Forest Service contract? If Johnson gets that contract all of Buster's employees would go to work for Johnson—or at least that's what Johnson said."

Stan flinched. Joe watched curiously as the older man cleared his throat, then spoke slowly, in a low voice. "The Forest Service contracts are extremely valuable to mills because without them, loggers are forced to cut private lands only. Private landowners are usually only interested in a quick profit, so they don't replant their forests properly, and mill owners don't get as good a harvest. You know about the contract Buster and Johnson were competing for."

"Yes, but I guess we didn't realize just how important a contract could be," Frank answered.

Joe sat and slowly shook his head. Could Bo Johnson have wanted the Forest Service contract badly enough to kill for it?

"Vance Galen did see Collins's car near Horizon just before the explosion," Callie reminded them softly.

Frank nodded. "But we don't have proof. If only we could look through Johnson's office."

"How can you do that?" Stan asked.

Joe knew what Frank was thinking. And he could see by Callie's expression that she knew, too.

"No," she said in a low voice. "You're not thinking of breaking into Bo Johnson's office—"

"You'd better not," Stan Shaw spoke up. "If Johnson caught you he'd—"

"It's okay, Stan," Frank said. "We don't have to decide right now." But Joe knew that, dangerous or not, Johnson's office was next on the agenda.

"Anyway, it's too late to do anything now," Joe said, stretching his arms and yawning. The reporters' voices had faded away outside. Joe guessed they'd given up and gone home.

"Let's get some sleep," Frank agreed, grinning innocently at a suspicious Stan Shaw. "We'll talk about it again tomorrow."

"About time you got up," Callie remarked the next morning as Joe stumbled into the kitchen, sat down at the table, and began ladling bacon and eggs onto his plate. "Stan's already checked in with the sheriff and had a talk with the home office, and Frank and I are ready to start the day. What's your contribution?"

"I'll be the driver," Joe suggested, pouring himself a large glass of juice. "And give those reporters out there the slip."

"Well, hurry up," Frank said, glancing at Stan. "It's nine-thirty, and we need to get to the general store in time to interview some of Owens's crew."

Joe nodded. He knew Frank's remark had been meant to put Stan's mind at ease. Frank and Joe intended to search Johnson's mill that day, but Callie had insisted they not tell her uncle.

Frank had agreed that Stan would worry too much, and besides, the environmentalist's reluctance to confide in them completely about his relationship with Buddy Owens had made Frank wonder what Stan was hiding.

The day's plan, Joe had learned the night before, was simple. They were to arrive at Bo Johnson's lumbermill just as the trucks arrived with the first deliveries of the day. They would park the jeep outside the mill's fence. While Frank talked to the guard about applying for a job, Joe and Callie would search any logging trucks parked outside for hard hats and safety goggles. The Hardys and Callie would borrow enough lumberjack equipment to look like real loggers. Then they'd drive to the back of the mill property and climb over the fence, and they'd be in.

That morning, Joe observed, the three of them seemed to be operating under a lucky star. They evaded all the reporters and before noon found themselves in the woods bordering the back of Bo Johnson's mill.

"Now we put on the goggles and hats," Callie announced, pulling her hair up into a ponytail and covering it with the yellow hard hat. "Remember—don't talk to anyone. All we want to do is search the office, have a look around the mill grounds, and get out fast."

"Okay," Joe said skeptically, slipping his goggles on and adjusting the hard hat to fit his head. "I just hope we make it through this. I'm not eager to get on familiar terms with Rafe Collins's fists."

"Neither are we," Frank assured him, fitting his hat to his head and peering through the chain-link fence at a small shack set far back from the other buildings.

"That must be where they keep the dynamite they use for blasting snags and stumps," Joe guessed, pointing at the shed. "They'd keep it out here in case of an accidental explosion."

"Right," said Frank. "Maybe I should borrow a stick while we're here. It might match what was in Stan's truck."

"Aren't you getting a little ahead of yourself?" Joe asked. But one look at Frank's face told him where his brother was headed.

"Okay," he said. "Callie and I can look for the office."

Frank gave Callie a boost over the seven-foot fence, then climbed over himself. Joe followed quickly.

"We'll meet back here in half an hour," Frank

said to his brother, "whether or not we find anything. Agreed?"

Joe gave Frank the thumbs-up sign before he and Callie hurried off.

It took almost fifteen minutes for Joe and Callie to discover that Bo Johnson's office was inside the main building of the mill. As they moved among the giant pieces of equipment inside, no one seemed to notice them.

Joe had never been in a working lumbermill before and was fascinated by the enormous wood chipper. As big as a small house, the chipper had an enormous mouth that was fed by a long conveyer belt on which workers tossed wood scrap and bark.

The roar the chipper made as it ground the scrap to bits was so loud that it drove all rational thoughts out of Joe's head. He was glad Callie had spotted the office and was already moving toward it.

As Joe moved along beside the conveyer belt, one of the goggled workers called out to him, "Hey, kid!"

Joe froze in his tracks and turned to face the man with heavy cotton gloves who was ripping branches from a pine trunk.

"You new here?" the man shouted over the noise.

Joe nodded. "I just started today," he yelled back.

"That so?" The worker turned to a man working beside him. "The lay-offs must be over if Johnson's hiring again."

Joe thought fast. "I'm just here for inventory," he shouted. "It's only temporary."

Just then someone farther down the line bellowed out something. Joe and the other workers spun around to see what was wrong.

"Punch the button! Punch the button!" a man was shouting, waving his arms at the others and pointing toward the gaping entrance of the chipper.

Joe swiveled around, then gasped. A body, lying half on and half off the conveyer belt, was partially hidden by the piles of debris. Joe peered through the dusty air at the unmoving figure.

"Frank!" he shouted, and raced for the mouth of the horrible machine.

The chipper could suck in massive pieces of wood and reduce them to splinters in mere seconds. Frank would be next, Joe realized as he raced the length of the conveyer belt. A large red emergency-stop button was placed prominently at the end of the belt, but Joe knew that he'd never get there in time. I have to! he told himself. Or Frank will be killed!

Chapter

12

"FRANK!" Joe screamed.

Frank's eyes fluttered open, and the entire room burst into motion. The mill workers who had been frozen, staring in shock, suddenly scrambled for the emergency button. The cavernous building was filled with screams and shouts.

The man closest to the button slammed his fist against it. The chipper ceased to grind, and the mill became silent. Slowly Frank moved and sat up.

"Frank!" Joe shouted, racing to his brother's side.

"What happened?" Joe gingerly touched a nasty cut on Frank's jaw. "Somebody got you good."

"Search me," said Frank, still dazed. "I was just about to climb into that shed when some-

111

body spun me around and a fist was rammed into my face. It happened so fast I didn't even see who did it."

Frank was interrupted by a loud voice nearby. "Who are these people?" the voice demanded.

Frank looked up to see Bo Johnson, his features drawn into an angry grimace as he surveyed the scene.

"You don't work here," Johnson said. "You're trespassing!"

"You're right, Mr. Johnson," Frank agreed, hoping for inspiration. "We sneaked in on a dare. We always wanted to see what a real lumbermill looked like."

"Well, you certainly have," Johnson snapped, obviously still furious. "You kids can't wander onto private property with dangerous machinery and then expect to be protected by the law. I want you off my property at once!"

Johnson glanced around, then snapped his long fingers at a pair of beefy workers. "Get them out of here," he ordered. "But confiscate those hard hats and goggles first. And, boys, if I ever see you on my property again, I'll call the sheriff *before* I come out to hear your lame excuses!"

As Frank and Joe were marched out of the sawmill, they looked everywhere for Callie. She was nowhere in sight. Frank hoped she had escaped while the crew had been distracted.

As they walked, Frank recognized several faces from the Sportsman's Pool Hall and the crowd at the Horizon fire. Then he noticed some-one more surprising. "Look over there," he said to Joe.

"Freddy Zackarias," Joe said, following Frank's gaze. "I thought he was just fired from Horizon."

"Well, he got a job here pretty quick," Frank said. "Maybe too quick."

"Shut up, you two," their guard growled, giving Frank a shake. "You can talk all you want when you get out of here."

When they reached the front gate, the guards demanded the borrowed equipment back. Frank and Joe handed over the hard hats and goggles happily.

"And stay out!" the first guard added as the boys walked through the gate. Frank turned and gave the guard a thumbs-up sign.

"All right," he said to his brother as they walked down the road to their jeep. "Now we figure out how to rescue Callie."

"No need," a voice called out.

Frank peered past a lumber truck to their jeep. Callie was sitting in the backseat, smiling out at him.

"Callie! How'd you get here?" Frank asked.

"You guys provided the perfect distraction," she said. "As soon as I saw you were okay, I slipped inside the office when no one was look-ing. I had a couple of minutes all to myself."

"Did you find anything?" Joe asked as the boys climbed into the jeep.

"Yeah," she said. "I did. In fact, I think it tells us what Uncle Stan wouldn't tell about Buster."

"Oh, yeah?" Frank backed the jeep out. "Don't keep us in suspense."

As Frank steered the jeep down the mountain road, out of sight of Johnson Lumber, Callie passed a sheaf of papers up to Frank and Joe.

"What's this?" Joe asked, examining the top page.

"A plan," said Callie, grinning like the Cheshire cat, "to completely reorganize a logging operation, including new equipment designed to cut new-growth timber—"

"New-growth timber?" Frank asked.

"Most mills are designed to cut tall, old trees, like Douglas firs," Callie explained briefly. "But they're the ones that the Greens want to save most. The loggers say it costs too much to have their equipment redesigned to cut up smaller trunks—or new growth—from replanted land," she went on. "But this plan describes a way to work it so everyone's happy—especially the Forest Service."

"The Forest Service?" Frank perked up, meeting Callie's gaze in the rearview mirror. "You mean this is a plan to win the Forest Service contract."

"Exactly," Callie said excitedly. "It has specifications on the new equipment and how long it would take to pay for itself—assuming that the company wins the contract. And it describes how to leave pockets of undisturbed forest with no added cost. *And* it tells how the mill can replace the trees it cuts down by getting the federal government to provide seedlings and planting expertise for free. And if the mill is willing to replant, the Forest Service guys are super-happy. So happy, in fact, they would probably agree to award an exclusive contract to all their forest land to the company that can offer these guarantees."

"Buster's and your uncle's plan," Joe said.

"Exactly," agreed Callie. "And it has my uncle's mark all over it. A perfect compromise that makes everyone happy."

"Everyone except Bo Johnson," Frank pointed out.

"Right." Callie leaned forward between the two front seats. "Johnson obviously got hold of a copy of the plan somehow—"

"Freddy Zackarias," Joe said quickly. "He was fired for going through Owens's office, and today we saw him hanging around Johnson's mill."

"Johnson must have realized that if Owens won that contract, he would be forced out of business," Frank interjected. "He couldn't let that happen and he killed Owens."

"It's more likely that he paid Collins to do the actual dirty work for him, though. Where to now?" Joe asked.

"The Crosscut *Guardian*'s offices," Frank said. "We need proof. I'd like to make prints from the photos I took near the bulldozer yesterday and compare them with the prints from around Buster's truck.''

"Step on it, Frank," Callie said. "I smell a solution coming."

Frank glanced, amused, at his passenger. "Yes, boss," he said, and pressed down on the accelerator. "After the detective work you did, your wish is our command."

"There you are!" Ronnie Croft said when the Hardys and Callie trooped into her office through the back door fifteen minutes later. "I was wondering what happened to you. The town's loaded with reporters, all demanding that I produce Stan Shaw for nonstop interviews."

"We saw a couple outside here," Callie said. "That's why we came in the back way. Last night they were all outside Uncle Stan's house. Fortunately, we were able to give them the slip when we left his house this morning."

"Now—don't tell me—you want to use my darkroom," Ronnie said.

"Actually, yes," Frank replied. "We need to make some more prints in a hurry. We think we might be near a solution to the case."

"In that case, help yourselves," Ronnie said eagerly. "But on one condition."

Frank hesitated on his way to the darkroom. "What's that?"

"If you *do* solve this case, and Stan Shaw's no longer a suspect, and every reporter in this town wants to interview you and Callie and Joe—"

"Yes?" Callie asked, grinning.

"You have to give me an exclusive interview."

"It's a deal," Frank said with a laugh.

In the dim amber light Joe and Callie peered at the row of photographs Frank had just printed. "Do you see anything yet?" Callie asked Frank.

"I'm not sure." Frank finished focusing the negative, turned the enlarger off, and slipped an eight-by-ten sheet of photographic paper over the enlarger's base. Then he turned on the enlarger light for a number of seconds, switched it off, and transferred the paper to the first vat of chemicals.

"This one seems promising," he said as he moved the photograph into the tray of fixer. "As soon as you hang it up we'll turn on the lights and take a closer look."

Five minutes later, Frank was standing on a stool in the now brightly lit room, peering at the photographs through a magnifying glass. Ronnie, Callie, and Joe were flanking him, trying to make out details in the prints.

"I still don't get it," Ronnie said impatiently. "What exactly are we looking for?"

"Something unusual in one of the bootprints," Joe explained. "If he finds a unique pattern in a print from near the bulldozer and can match it with a print from beside Owens's car, then that means the same person was in both places. And *that* means—"

"Once you match the bootprint to someone's boot, you have a good chance of being able to name the murderer." Ronnie tossed her hair back over her shoulder.

"I hope you find something," Callie said anxiously. "There's only one more day till that arson report comes back. And since it seems pretty certain that that dynamite is from the same batch that was planted on Uncle Stan, he'll probably be arrested immediately."

"Joe, look at this," Frank said suddenly, pulling back from one of the photographs and hurriedly unclipping it. He handed the magnifying glass to Joe, then climbed down from the stool and strode over to the filing cabinet in the corner, where he'd left extra prints from the earlier printing session.

Frank grabbed one of the earlier photographs and brought it over beside the new one. "Compare them," he said to his brother, barely able to control the excitement in his voice.

Slowly and deliberately, Joe peered through the glass at first one photograph, then the other. He turned to his brother and said with a gleam in his eyes, "I think you did it, Frank.

"See," Joe explained to Callie and Ronnie, "there are three hobnails missing in a little triangle down on this side." He pointed to the bootprint in the newer photo. Then he moved the magnifying glass over to the older print. "And here it is again. Three missing nails in exactly the same place.''

"Frank!" Callie looked up from the magnifying glass, her face alight with excitement. "You really did it! Now if we can find the boot to match these prints, Uncle Stan's practically free!"

Chapter

13

FRANK AND JOE gathered up the photographs and stacked them into piles.

"I have a feeling we'll find those boots on Rafe Collins's feet." Joe handed his stack to Frank.

"You might have some trouble persuading him to take them off," Callie pointed out.

"Collins did the dirty work for Johnson, and Johnson may not have been fooled by our act at the mill," Joe pointed out. "He might have sent Collins after us already."

"We need to get Uncle Stan's advice. He knows these people best," Callie said. "Besides, I want to ask him why he kept his plan with Owens a secret."

Joe turned to Ronnie, who was standing, silently taking everything in. "You really think Bo

Johnson's responsible for Owens's death?'' she demanded excitedly.

Frank held up a hand to stop her. "Remember that interview. Well, if you're quiet, you get it. If you tell, you don't."

She held the back door open for them, and they sneaked back out into the cool afternoon air.

Stan Shaw gave a low whistle as he looked over Frank's stack of photos in his kitchen less than half an hour later. "These are great pictures, Frank," Stan said. "And it's a good thing. They might save me."

"The trouble is, we still have to find this boot to prove who committed both crimes," Frank said excitedly.

"Rafe Collins isn't the type who'll let us examine his footwear," Joe pointed out wryly. "And we're practically positive that Collins is our guy."

"My suggestion, then, is to give these photographs to the sheriff," Stan said. "He could have Collins brought in for questioning and impound his logging boots as evidence."

"We will," Callie assured him. "But first we need to do a few things to make our case as foolproof as possible."

"Like what?" Stan asked, accepting a tuna sandwich that Joe had made.

"Like ask you why you refused to tell us about the Forest Service plan you had worked out with Buster Owens," Frank said, taking a sandwich and joining Stan and Callie at the table.

Stan's gaze switched to Callie.

"We found a copy of the plan," she explained nervously. "In Bo Johnson's office."

Stan slammed down his sandwich. "You were in Johnson's office? You could have been killed!"

"We had to go, Uncle Stan!" Callie protested. "You wouldn't tell us what you and Owens were meeting about. And it did turn out to be important!"

Stan stared at his niece for a moment. Then his gaze dropped to the table. "I should have told you. The only reason Buster was willing to change over to conservation-friendly equipment was to put Johnson out of business. Actually that was all right with us because all along, Johnson has violated just about every environmentally supportive law on the books. He really would shave these mountains clean and leave nothing but stumps. Buster wasn't much better at first, but at least he was willing to try—especially if it hurt Johnson. His only requirement for taking the risk was that I not say a word until it went through. He was afraid that his loggers would quit and join Johnson if they knew."

"But after he died, why couldn't you tell us then?"

Stan shook his head. "I wanted to. But I didn't want to squeal. I was hoping Millie would come around to her father's way of thinking, and I didn't want her to lose her crews. Please believe me—I never imagined that the plan could have anything to do with Buster's death. Is there any other evidence that Collins might have committed the murder?"

"Yeah," replied Joe. "Your assistant, Vance Galen, spotted Collins's car, that old red Caddie, near Buster's truck just minutes before the explosion took place."

Stan's eyes widened. "Why didn't he tell me?"

"He's afraid of Johnson and Collins," Callie said. "And he thinks the sheriff won't believe him."

"I need to speak with him," Stan said, reaching for the phone. "He's in grave danger if Collins or Johnson is guilty and they even suspect that Galen knows. I'm afraid they're not the only ones around here who would be relieved to see him go."

Stan dialed Galen's number, but no one answered. Finally Stan replaced the receiver in its cradle.

"He might just not be answering his phone," Frank pointed out. "He was pretty spooked last time we saw him."

"I say we pay him another visit," Joe decided.

"You're right," Callie said.

"Can you distract those reporters?" Frank asked Stan. The older man nodded.

"We'll be back in an hour or two," he told

him. "And if we're not, send someone, like the sheriff, to find us."

"I wonder if the bulldozer will still be there," Callie said from the backseat as the jeep powered up the road on Stoner Mountain.

Joe stared out at the road. "I doubt it. Didn't Walter Ecks say he'd return it to the equipment yard?"

"I kept an eye out for strangers," Frank remarked. "That guy in camouflage who attacked Joe might still be— What's that?" he interrupted himself as he was staring out the window.

"What?" Callie swiveled around to look.

"There was a truck parked on a logging road leading off into the woods," Frank said, turning around as well. "Yes, there it is!" he added as a truck came into view in the distance. "I think we're being followed!"

"Don't get paranoid." Joe glanced in his rearview mirror. "We're not the only people allowed to drive on this mountain, you know."

"Yeah, but how many local folks lie in ambush for our jeep to pass by?" Frank pointed out. "Speed up," he added. "Let's do some ambushing ourselves. If it's nobody we know, at least we'll have gotten to Galen's place a little faster."

"Whatever you say." Joe pressed his foot down on the accelerator.

The jeep bolted up the mountain. It flew over

a bump in the road and rounded a corner practically on two wheels.

Joe glanced into his rearview mirror again. "They're lost," he reported. "If they were ever found, that is."

"Turn off there," Frank ordered, pointing to a barely visible logging road.

"Aye-aye, sir." Joe slammed on the brakes and made a sharp right turn onto the muddy road. The jeep swerved wildly. Joe pumped the brakes again and the jeep made a 180-degree skid to face the main road.

Moments later the truck appeared, driving very slowly up the mountain as though the driver was searching for something. "Here he comes," Frank said in a soft voice. "When I give the word, block the road."

Joe kept his eyes on the truck. When Frank said, "Now," Joe slammed the car into gear and punched the accelerator.

The jeep roared out of the woods like a wild animal, heading straight toward the slow-moving truck.

Through the truck's windshield, Joe could see Freddy Zackarias scream. Frantically, the logger spun the steering wheel. But he lost control, and the truck careened off the side of the road and onto the cliff beside it.

"Is he hurt?" Callie asked as Joe pulled up next to the truck and hopped out. Freddy, in camouflage, sat inside, rubbing his forehead.

"Bruised a little," said Joe. "But compared to what we've been through lately, it's nothing."

"End of the line, Freddy," Frank was saying as he leaned in the window of the truck. "Hey, what's this?"

Frank reached past Freddy to retrieve something from the seat beside him. "Look," he said, holding a walkie-talkie up for Joe and Callie to see. "It says 'Property of Johnson Lumber' right here on the back."

"What do you want?" Freddy asked. He was glaring, but Joe saw fear in his eyes.

"Answers," Joe replied. "Why were you following us?"

"I wasn't. I was just going in the same direction," Freddy said.

"Uh-uh, Freddy," Frank replied, leaning his arms on the window frame of Freddy's truck and peering inside. "Somebody's been reporting our movements to Bo Johnson, and that somebody is you."

"I don't know what you're—" Freddy began defensively.

"Save it," Joe snapped. "We know you're Johnson's spy. How long have you been on our tail today? Since we left the sawmill?"

"You can't prove anything!" Freddy shouted at them.

"If I were you, I'd be scared they'd bump me off because I knew too much," Frank added.

"And if you helped Collins kill Buster Owens, that makes you an accessory to murder," Callie

126

pointed out. "I wonder how many years you'll get?"

"Ready, gang?" Joe asked, satisfied. As soon as Frank and Callie were back in the jeep, he stepped on the gas. Freddy's truck disappeared as the jeep rounded a bend.

"He might go right back to Collins and Johnson and tell them what we said," Frank remarked as they neared the top of the mountain.

"Great," said Joe. "How will that help us?"

"It might spook Collins and Johnson into doing something careless," Frank replied. "And then maybe we can catch them in the act."

"Are you sure we want to risk that?" Callie asked. "Stan was pretty worried that those guys would figure out what we were up to."

"Too late now," Joe pointed out. "If we didn't want them to know what we were up to, we never should have shown up at Bo Johnson's mill."

"Finally, we're at Walt Ecks's house. Straight grade to Vance's place. Now if we can just—"

Joe never heard the rest of Frank's sentence. In that instant a shot rang out.

"Duck!" Callie screamed.

Before Joe could even react, a bullet shattered the windshield.

Chapter

14

AS CALLIE SCREAMED, Frank pushed her head down and then ducked under the dashboard himself. He felt the jeep veer wildly to the right and lurch into a nearby field.

"Joe?" he yelled as the jeep rolled to a stop. There was nothing but silence.

"Joe!" Frank shouted as he reached over the gearshift for his brother.

"Yeah, yeah. I'm okay."

Frank sank back, relieved.

"But I think I got some glass in my forehead."

"You're lucky," Callie said from behind Joe's seat. "Somebody isn't kidding around."

"And we're sitting ducks," Frank added. "Joe, when I give the word, throw open your door, then you and Callie slide over and get out the passenger-side door."

"What about our playmate with the rifle?" Joe asked.

"He should be shooting at your door," Frank explained. "It's our only chance, so let's do it. Ready? One, two, now!"

Frank knew his ruse had worked when the sniper put several rounds through the driver's door. By the time the gunman realized his error, Frank, Joe, and Callie had already scrambled into the underbrush beside the road.

"Who *is* that guy?" Callie whispered, clutching Frank by the arm as they crouched in the bushes, trying to catch their breath.

"What difference does it make?" whispered Joe, who hid a few feet from them.

Frank heard three shots ring out. The ground only five feet from their hiding place exploded. Callie stifled a shriek and huddled closer to Frank.

"That was too close," Frank said, feeling himself break out into a clammy sweat. "Move into the woods. Fast!"

Frank crawled on hands and knees to where the forest began. Glancing back to make sure Callie was right behind him, he dove into the darkness of the trees, then got to his feet and ran.

Despite the afternoon sun, it was dark beneath the trees. After only fifty yards Frank tripped over a trailing vine. Callie, right behind him, tripped over Frank, and Joe tripped over them both. Lying still, Callie whispered tensely, "Okay. What do we do now?"

"We could try splitting up and attacking the guy from two different directions," Joe suggested.

"What are we going to attack him with?" Frank asked impatiently. "Rocks?"

Before Joe could reply, Frank heard shots ring out from somewhere up the road. "Wait," he whispered in the silence that followed, "wasn't that a different gun?"

The *crack-whiz!* sounds of the second rifle's shots were answered by the familiar boom of the sniper's hunting rifle.

"It sounds like a gun battle!" Frank said, bewildered. "What's going on?"

"Maybe it's the sheriff," Callie suggested. The three of them listened a moment longer. The gunmen were definitely shooting at each other.

"Let's circle back to the road," Joe suggested.

"Right," Frank agreed. "But be careful. We don't want to get caught in crossfire!"

Frank crept behind Callie through the thick woods as she followed Joe. When they reached the bushes that lined the road, they paused to make sure the coast was clear.

Just as Joe started to lead them out onto the road, a car came tearing around the bend in the road. Joe froze.

"Joe!" Callie squealed helplessly.

The car slowed and the driver's head appeared through the windshield. To Frank's relief he recognized the face.

"It's Walter!" he said to Callie. "Walter Ecks!"

Walter pulled the station wagon off the road, and Joe, Callie, and Frank raced toward the doors and began climbing in. "Watch out!" Frank said to Walter. "There's a sniper out there!"

"I know!" Automatically, Ecks ducked down to the floor along with the others. A moment later he said, "I heard the shooting from my cabin! Is anybody hurt?"

"We're okay, thanks," Frank replied as the four of them cautiously rose a little in their seats. Frank realized that there was a pump shotgun on the seat beside the driver.

"Who was shooting at you?" Ecks demanded.

"We don't know," Callie replied. "But we heard two guns. Did you fire?"

Ecks's answer was drowned out by a wave of noise that suddenly surrounded the car. Before Frank knew what was happening, Walter Ecks was out of the station wagon, his shotgun aimed over the roof of the car at a very surprised Vance Galen. In one hand Galen held a .22 rifle.

"Don't shoot!" Galen shouted. "It was me who drove the sniper off. Anybody hurt?"

"No," Joe answered from inside the station wagon, "but our jeep got shot up."

"Did you see the sniper?" Frank asked Vance.

"Just a glimpse. It was somebody in camouflage perched in a tree." Galen made his way through the brush to the car. "I never got a clear look at him."

"You heard shots from your place, I guess," Ecks said suspiciously, lowering his own rifle very slowly.

"Yeah, so I came running. Then I saw your jeep and I knew something was up."

Ecks looked in the car at the three shaken teenagers. "Who'd want to go after you?" he asked.

"We think it has to do with Buster's murder," Frank told him.

"Somebody must have figured we were coming to see you or Vance, and they wanted to keep us from asking questions," Joe added.

Ecks sighed wearily. "I think we'd better go see the sheriff," he said. "We've got one fine person dead already. No use in more of us following."

"You're right, sir." Frank turned pointedly to Vance Galen. "It's time we all talked to Ferris."

"Will you talk to Ferris now, Vance?" Callie asked, her eyes searching his face.

"Yes!" Galen said. "I've had enough of this violence!"

"And, sir," Frank added to Walter Ecks, "you should tell him about the bulldozer being taken."

Ecks nodded. "Sure, if you think it will help. I want to get the guys who killed Buster."

"Why don't you take Vance into town?" Frank suggested. "Tell Ferris we'll be in soon."

"Where are you going?" Galen asked.

"Relax," Frank assured him. "We're going

out to find a piece of evidence that may just solve the case."

"Where *are* we going, Frank?" Joe asked as the two men drove off in Ecks's car.

"We're going to find Collins's car," Frank replied. "Maybe there's something in it that will link Collins to the murder."

"How are we going to find it?" Callie asked. "Even if Collins was the guy who shot at us, he could be anywhere by now."

"My guess is that Collins headed for someplace where witnesses could vouch for his presence. A place like Johnson Lumber," Frank speculated. "He probably needs to tell Johnson what's happening, anyway."

Joe frowned. "I guess it's as good a place to look as any. But what if Collins's car isn't there?"

"Then we give Ferris the evidence and information we have already, and hope it's enough."

It took nearly half an hour to clean up the jeep and check the tires for punctures. When they finished, it was nearly five o'clock.

"Look for a red Cadillac convertible," Frank said as they pulled up to the far end of the Johnson lumberyard's parking lot. The three of them scanned the lot, but the Cadillac wasn't there.

"Now what?" said Callie.

"Now you go ask the guard where Collins is," Frank said simply.

"I what?"

"Tell him you're his parole officer. You need to have him sign some papers right away, or he's in big trouble. Act angry," Frank said, fighting a grin.

Callie hesitated. "I don't look much like a parole officer after rolling around in the mud," she pointed out.

"Come on, Callie, we have faith in you," Joe prodded, grinning. "The guards will never recognize you without a hard hat on. We'll wait here."

Shaking her head, Callie climbed out of the backseat and headed across the parking lot toward the guard's post by the gate. A few minutes later she was back again. Frank was amused to see her walking primly, with a frown on her face, as though she'd taken on the character of a parole officer and now she couldn't shake it off.

"Where to, boss?" Frank asked as Joe put the jeep into gear.

"Sector eight," Callie answered mysteriously. "Collins is out inspecting log flumes. I know the sectors from inspecting the forests with Uncle Stan. They're numbered one through ten, with number one closest to the mill. Go straight on the access road until I tell you to turn."

As they drove along the muddy, heavily rutted road, Frank looked for Collins's red Caddy. "I can't wait to return this jeep to the rental counter now," Joe remarked glumly as he, too, searched through the trees. "Let's see, should we tell them a plane wandered off its flight path and flew straight through our windshield? Or maybe the Abominable Snowman turned up and sat on it."

"Don't worry," said Frank. "If we solve this case the rental agent will know who we are. And of course we'll pay for any damage not covered by the insurance."

"Sssh!" Callie interrupted, staring to the right and ahead of the car. "There it is!"

Following Callie's orders, Joe turned right onto a still narrower dirt road. The Cadillac was parked beside a tractor-trailer loaded with metal pipes. The big truck sat next to a large trestle of wood and steel that supported a V-shaped wooden log flume that logs sped down on their way to the sawmill.

"Wow, I've never seen one of these outside an amusement park," Joe said. Frank studied how the flume was built beside a creek that flowed down toward the sawmill. A mechanical pump channeled water into the flume, so that even the largest logs could float down the V-shaped wooden tray to the sawmill. They picked up speed as they coursed downhill.

"I don't see Collins," Frank said to Joe. "Callie, keep a lookout. Let's get to work, fast!"

As Frank and Joe clambered out of the jeep and ran over to the Cadillac, Callie climbed onto the roof of the tractor-trailer's cab to get a better view of the surrounding forest.

"Any blood on the backseat?" Frank asked Joe as he reached beneath the driver's seat, finding nothing.

"No. If he took Buster to the Horizon mill in here, he must have put a blanket under him," Joe replied. Then he added, "Bingo! Frank, I found it!"

Frank raised his head over the front seat to see Joe kneeling on the floor behind him. He'd opened a metal tool chest that was stashed behind the driver's seat. The top tray was removed, and Joe held a shiny object half-wrapped in an oily rag.

"What is it?" Frank demanded.

Gleefully, Joe shook the object until the rag fell back, revealing the find to Frank.

"The key ring!" Frank said, a grin spreading across his face. "We've got Collins now, Joe!"

"Not quite!" growled a low voice.

The hair rose on the back of Frank's neck as he slowly turned toward the voice. He knew without looking what he'd find there.

It was Rafe Collins, in camouflage, standing beside the trailer load of pipes. He was pointing a rifle straight at Frank. Frank stared at Collins's index finger as it tightened on the trigger.

Chapter

15

"GET OUT OF THE CAR," Collins told Frank and Joe. "Don't make any sudden moves."

The Hardys stared at the angry, hawk-nosed man in the dim light of the forest. Behind him, Joe glimpsed Callie's hand waving to get the boys' attention from the far end of the trailer truck.

Frank's intent, watchful expression revealed that he had noticed Callie, too.

"Let's go," Collins barked. "I don't want to get any bullet holes in my Cadillac."

"Looks like it could use a little work," Joe muttered as, hands up, he stepped out of the car. "I guess this mountain life just isn't good for it."

Collins stared at him, unsure whether Joe had insulted him or not. "You've got a smart mouth,

137

kid," he said at last. "You'd better watch out or I just might shut it for you."

"Don't you have to ask Johnson's permission first?" Frank asked pointedly.

Joe watched as Collins's squinty eyes got even narrower. "Keep talking, wiseguys," Collins muttered. "You're only making it worse for yourselves."

Joe kept stalling so that Callie could make her move. "You're in a big hurry to shoot us, aren't you, Collins? You think that's going to solve all your problems?"

"That would be a big mistake," Frank said, following Joe's lead. "At least before you find out who we've talked to and what we told them."

"Shut up!" Collins exploded. Waving the rifle back and forth between them, he snarled, "Where's the girl?"

Joe saw Callie make an "okay" sign with her thumb and forefinger from atop the pipes at the far end of the trailer. Then she stood up and shoved with all her strength on the end of one pipe.

"All right!" Joe shouted. The pipe shot out and struck Collins on the right shoulder, sending him pitching forward. As Collins stumbled to his knees, his rifle swung up. Joe pounced.

"Grab the rifle!" he yelled at his brother as he grappled with the man on the forest floor. Frank leapt forward and grabbed the barrel of the rifle. Wrestling it upward, Frank tried to force the rifle out of Collins's hands. But in the next instant the foreman sent Joe flying with one arm and shoved the rifle stock into Frank's stomach with the other.

With a grunt, Frank collapsed like a sack of potatoes.

"Joe!" Callie called from the top of the trailer.

Dazed, Joe looked up from where he'd fallen to watch, horrified, as Collins lifted his rifle and aimed it directly at Frank.

Joe leapt to his feet and fell onto Collins's back, sending him sprawling sideways with the rifle an arm's length away.

"Watch it, Collins!" Joe taunted, grabbing the rifle and flinging it into the bushes. "You almost hurt yourself!" He danced from side to side, trying to draw attention away from his brother.

"So you got rid of my gun, eh?" Collins growled. "That's okay." Collins staggered toward Joe. "A knife fight's more my style anyway."

Whipping a knife out of a leather sheath that hung from his belt, Collins feinted at Joe. Joe jumped back, and the ex-convict slashed his knife sideways in a glittering, underhanded sweep that missed Joe's stomach by inches.

"Especially if the other guy doesn't have one," Joe retorted. He danced backward, farther and farther away from Frank. Collins took the bait, running after Joe and slashing the air between them with his gleaming blade.

"Frank! Callie! Get out of here!" Joe shouted

as he worked his way backward, always a step from Collins's vicious slashes. Behind Collins, Joe watched as Callie raced over to Frank and helped him up.

"Run for the jeep!" Joe called as he moved away from the flashing blade.

Collins spun around to see Callie and Frank getting away. Enraged, he charged toward them, cutting off their path to the jeep.

Joe ran after Collins as fast as he could. Just as he was prepared to lunge at the foreman again, though, Collins turned and brandished the knife in his face.

"Come on, kid," Collins shouted. "Try me!"

As Joe and Collins circled each other in a deadly game of tag, Joe's eye was caught by a group of tree trunks floating quickly down the flume. They gave him an idea.

"Frank, Callie, run to the log flume! Ride a log to get away!" Joe shouted.

Keeping himself between Collins and Frank and Callie, Joe backed toward the flume. He circled to avoid Collins's blade, glancing repeatedly over his shoulder until the flume came into full view.

Frank, weak but determined, was already standing on the edge of the two-foot-deep flume. As Joe watched in quick glimpses, Frank and Callie jumped aboard the next log that rumbled by. Holding their arms out and keeping their legs flexed for balance, they slid down the man-made stream. Collins moved forward again, and Joe lost sight of them as he concentrated on getting away.

"It's all right, kid," Collins growled as he tried to force Joe back against a pine tree. "They can get away. I still have you to hold hostage."

"You wish, Collins," Joe said, ducking out of the foreman's reach. The flume was only a few steps behind him now. "When I get out of here I'm going straight to the sheriff," Joe taunted. "Your days of freedom are numbered."

Just before Joe reached the flume, Collins made a quick lunge at him. Joe slammed a karate chop down on Collins's wrist. But the blow failed to knock the knife loose from his hand. Doubly enraged, Collins now charged at the boy with his knife raised above his head.

A sudden roaring noise warned Joe that another log was on its way down. He turned in time to see the huge log appear in the flume. As it passed, Joe sprang up and landed awkwardly on the slick bark, faced in the wrong direction.

Thrilled to get away from the deranged murderer, Joe maintained his balance and slowly turned around to face the front on the swiftly moving log.

"Cool," he said to himself as the dusky landscape surged past. "It's like catching a monster wave at the beach!"

Moments later the flume began to level out. Up ahead, Joe could see that it emptied into a dammed-up backwater. As Joe's log sped toward the pool of still water, Joe prepared for the rough landing. At the end of the flume, the log dropped out from under him, and Joe flew through the air to land in the water with a splash.

He sank down through the water, then bobbed back up to the surface. He shook the water out of his hair and hooted triumphantly. He spotted Frank and Callie watching from a huge log boom—a raft of five dozen huge tree trunks lashed together and chained to a spotlighted dock.

"We made it!" Joe cried as he swam toward them. "You were great, Callie!" He reached the edge of the boom and grabbed the nearest log to try to pull himself up. But the wood was too slippery.

"How about a hand here?" he called.

Joe was surprised when Frank and Callie didn't move to help him.

"Are you guys deaf? I asked for a hand up!"

As Joe tried to scramble up on the slippery log by himself, he saw that someone was standing up behind Callie and Frank.

It was Bo Johnson.

Johnson stepped nimbly over to Joe's log and whipped a snub-nosed revolver out of his belt.

"Sure, kid," he said as he shoved it in Joe's face. "I'll give you a hand—right into your grave!"

Joe cast a quick glance in Frank's direction.

A discreet nod told him Frank was ready for action.

"I can't get up," Joe said to Johnson in a casual voice. "Really—can you help me up?"

"Not a chance, kid," Johnson snapped. "I'm not that dumb."

"Let me help," Frank said quietly, taking a step toward Johnson.

Johnson wheeled around, pointing the gun at Frank. "Stay where you are!"

It was a perfect chance, and Joe took it. Pushing down on the log, he shot up out of the water, grabbed Johnson around the upper body, and pinned his arms to his sides. At the same time, Frank slammed into Johnson from the other side, and Joe, Frank, and Johnson fell backward into the dark green water of the millpond.

As soon as they hit the water, Frank was separated from his brother and the mill owner. For long, frightening seconds, he struggled to find them in the murky water beside the massive logs. Finally out of breath, he swam to the surface and saw his brother pop up at the same time. Callie cried out, "Joe! Watch out!" as Bo Johnson lunged at Joe from behind. Joe turned and struck out. He caught Johnson on the side of the head and watched as he fell backward, striking his head on a floating log. He slid silently beneath the surface of the water.

"Catch him!" Frank ordered. "Otherwise he'll drown."

Joe and Frank towed the unconscious sawmill

owner back toward the raft, where Callie stood watching. Frank kept Johnson afloat while Joe climbed onto the raft. Then he and Callie hauled Johnson aboard and laid him on his side. Johnson drew a deep, shuddery breath, then pushed himself up on his elbows.

Frank pulled himself up onto the raft and walked over to Johnson. "Can you stand, Mr. Johnson?" he asked as he helped him up. "Good. Then you can come with us to see Sheriff Ferris."

Johnson coughed again. "You'll never get me there."

"Who's going to stop us?" Joe asked as they led Johnson across the log boom toward the dock. "You can't, and your hired thug, Collins, is back up the mountain."

"Your first mistake was underestimating us, Johnson," Frank said. He quickly added, "Your second one was trying to frame a friend of ours. Now it's payback time."

"Don't be so sure your plans will work out so perfectly," Johnson said.

Callie interrupted. "How will we get out of here?"

"We'll use Johnson's car," Joe replied. "I'm sure he won't mind giving us a lift to Ferris's office."

In the distance Joe heard a car approaching. It sounded like someone was playing the radio. The sound grew louder and Joe spotted a large red car speeding down the access road to the dock.

"Here comes the cavalry," Johnson said smugly.

The red Cadillac squealed to a stop at the base of the dock, and Rafe Collins hopped out. Beaming at the Hardys, Collins went around to the trunk of the car, opened it, and pulled out a chainsaw with the longest blade Joe had ever seen.

"Howdy, kids!" he called as he reached forward to thumb the starter switch on. "It's woodshop time!"

As Callie and the Hardys stared in horror, the chainsaw started up with an ear-splitting roar.

Chapter

16

"SCATTER!" Frank ordered.

"What about Johnson?" Joe shouted.

"Forget Johnson!" Frank shouted back. "Save yourself!"

Collins jumped off the end of the dock and landed easily on the log boom. Frank stared in horror as he moved to within thirty feet of Joe, who stubbornly held on to Johnson.

Suddenly Johnson's elbow shot back and jabbed into Joe's stomach. Joe let go of Johnson and doubled over in pain. But Joe knew he had to act fast.

He straightened up and slammed Johnson in the jaw with a sudden uppercut. Silently Johnson collapsed to the floor of the raft.

The instant Johnson dropped, Collins charged Joe with the chainsaw. Callie screamed, but

Frank remained perfectly still, tensed for action. The big saw looked heavy, he observed, but Collins had the strength to swing its blade around in wide, dangerous slashes.

As Collins drew close to Joe, Frank's eyes darted around him in search of something to use as a weapon. At last he spotted two rusty peaveys leaning against the side of the dock. Six-foot poles topped with long pointed spikes and a bared hook, peaveys were used by loggers to manhandle the logs in the water. But Frank had another use for them.

Behind Collins's back, Frank dashed over to the peaveys, picking up one in each hand. "Catch, Joe!" he shouted, hurling the peavey in his left hand like a javelin. It sailed past Collins to Joe, who caught it in both hands.

Joe instantly turned the peavey against Collins, holding it out in front of him like a spear. With a laugh, Collins dodged the peavey's point and swung his chainsaw blade around to lop off its head. The sharp steel tip hit the log beneath their feet with a dull thud.

"Too bad, son!" Collins jeered as Joe retreated several steps, still holding the pole out before him. Collins slashed his sawblade in a Z-shaped pattern, cutting off another foot of Joe's pole. "Better give up now!"

Collins was so occupied with cornering Joe that he failed to notice Frank charging toward him from behind. Slamming the peavey straight down over Collins's shoulder, Frank used the peavey like a crowbar to pry the chainsaw from the foreman's hands.

Frank and Joe watched, fascinated, as the huge chainsaw went skidding over the edge of the log boom into the water and sank in a trail of oily bubbles.

"You!" Collins roared, turning his rage on Frank. But Frank was ready for him. He swung the peavey down on Collins's shoulder, then brought up the butt end of the pole and struck the foreman in the stomach. Callie and Joe watched, frozen, as Collins staggered backward into the pool.

"He's drowning!" Callie shouted as Frank and Joe watched Collins flounder in the water. Frank grabbed the peavey and snagged the collar of Collins's shirt with the hook.

"Had enough, Collins?" Frank asked.

Collins glared at the Hardys. Then he nodded sullenly.

The next morning Frank was still sore from the previous day's adventures as he sat at Sheriff Ferris's desk, sipping a soda. Joe sat on one side of Frank, with Callie on the other. Stan Shaw stood, leaning against the wall next to Callie.

"Now let me make sure I have all of this straight," Ferris was saying. "It was Rafe Collins who actually planted the dynamite in the Horizon sawmill."

"Right," Frank confirmed. "My guess is that

if you compare Johnson Lumber's dynamite with the results of the arson investigators' lab results that should arrive today, the two should match perfectly. And remember that Vance Galen saw Collins's red Cadillac by the mill just before it blew up."

"So far the story holds together," Ferris replied. "But how did Buster Owens end up in the Horizon mill?"

"First, you need to remember that Collins had Buster's key ring," Joe responded. "Millie Owens identified it herself, right?"

The sheriff nodded.

"That key ring could only have come from Buster," Joe continued. "Since Buster had the keys until at least an hour before he died, chances are that he killed Buster and stole the keys. And then there are the bootprints. Did you compare Collins's boots with those prints Frank photographed?"

"I certainly did, last night," the sheriff told the group. "The sole of one boot has three missing hobnails right where Frank's pictures showed them missing."

"Did you find Collins's fingerprints on the dynamite he planted in Stan Shaw's truck, or on the bulldozer he tried to ram us with?" Frank asked.

"Nope," Ferris told him. "He must have been wearing gloves. But the bootprints, along with the key ring and Galen's testimony, might be evidence enough."

"What I don't get is why Johnson framed *me*," Stan said mildly.

"Yeah. Vance Galen would seem a more likely person to pin it on," Joe agreed.

"But if Stan was being held by the sheriff as a murderer, it would give Johnson a better chance to get that franchise from the Forest Service. After all, that's what he was aiming for," Frank pointed out.

"You see, Sheriff," Frank went on, "we think that when Johnson learned what Buster was planning, he figured the only way to keep from being put out of business was to close down Horizon Lumber until *he* could retool at Johnson Lumber. That's why he tried to buy the equipment that was intended for Horizon."

"But why would he kill poor Buster?" Stan Shaw wondered.

"I'm not so sure killing Buster was part of the plan," Joe replied. "Judging by the way his truck was forced off the road some distance from the mill, Buster's running into Collins might have been an accident. Maybe Collins panicked when he realized Buster was headed for his mill, and forced him off the road. He knocked him out and then decided to eliminate him by leaving him in the mill."

"Well, all that's for a jury to decide," Ferris observed. "At least now the right people will be tried for the crimes. Stan, I'm sorry you had to go through all this."

"No hard feelings," Stan Shaw said with a

wan smile. "You were just doing your job. But if that's all you need, I'd like to get out of here."

"Of course," Ferris agreed as he stood up and opened his office door. "I guess I can get the rest of the story from Freddy Zackarias," Ferris said with a knowing chuckle. "Guess he was pretty busy acting as a spy for Collins. Collins wouldn't have known where you'd be without Freddy following you fellas. But I think Freddy's ready to testify against Collins and Johnson—he was in way over his head. Frank and Joe, you and Callie have been a big help. If I need more information—"

"We'll be happy to help, Sheriff," Frank replied as everyone headed for the door. "We'll be here in Crosscut for another week or so."

"Let's hit the Potbelly Café," Stan said as the weary group filed outside of the office. "I'm craving some of their fried chicken and biscuits. And to show you all how grateful I am, the meal's on me."

"Can't say no to that, can we, Frank?" said Joe with a wink.

"No way," Frank agreed. "But there's just one commitment we have to honor first."

"Oh?" Stan Shaw paused, looking puzzled. "What more commitments could you boys have?"

"A personal interview with Ronnie Croft," Frank started to explain. And, as Callie and Joe joined him, he added, "An exclusive!"

Frank and Joe's next case:

The Hardy boys have come to the Yucatán to take on a gang of grave robbers. Stolen Mexican artifacts have appeared in Bayport, and Frank and Joe intend to cut the smugglers off at the source. But the jungle is full of deception and distraction, including a bevy of beautiful models who have appeared at the site for a photo shoot.

A different kind of shooting, though, quickly puts the Hardys back on track. The raiders of the Mayan pyramids are not about to give up their lucrative looting without a fight. They plan to draw Frank and Joe into the jungle and add two deep new chambers to the ancient tombs . . . in *Grave Danger*, Case #61 in The Hardy Boys Casefiles™.